By Dean Murray

Reflections

Broken

Torn

Splintered

Intrusion

Numb

Trapped

Forsaken

Riven

Driven

Lost

Marked

Left

Dark Reflections

Bound

Hunted

Ambushed

Shattered

Burned

The Awakening

Reborn

Immortal

Endless

A Broken World

The Society

The Destroyer

The Warlord

The Founder

The Outsider

The Desolation

Reflections

(Dean Writing as Eldon)

The Greater Darkness

A Darkness Mirrored

The Compelled Chronicles

Stone Heart

The Guadel Chronicles

Frozen Prospects

Thawed Fortunes

I'rone

Brittle Bonds

Shattered Ties

Stone Heart

Dean Murray

Copyright © 2015 by Dean Murray

Published by Fir'shan Publishing

ISBN 978-1-9393635-6-5

www.FirshanPublishing.com

First Edition

For Shalese

For being sensitive to stuff that the rest of us don't notice.

Chapter 1

As I pulled up to the high school, I found myself hoping that there weren't too many cute boys in this town. I've always liked boys as much as any teenage girl, but things were more complicated for me than they were for my peers.

Things always started out okay—or at least what felt like okay to me—but it never lasted. The initial dates were all pretty easy. The guys pursued me without a whole lot of work on my part, and usually we had a lot of fun, but sooner or later—usually sooner—the guy always inexplicably lost interest in me.

I say always, but the truth is that it wasn't quite always. The decent guys, the ones who respected people's boundaries and weren't prone to stabbing their best friends in the back, lost interest. The jerks, on the other hand, seemed to just get more and more interested as time went on. It was like whatever drove the good guys away was catnip for the kind of guys that I knew I didn't actually want to date.

I'd been trying to figure out what was wrong with me since before I'd turned thirteen. I looked normal—neither too tall nor too short—with blond hair, blue eyes and a body that I kept in shape without letting exercise become an obsession like it did for some people. I even wore makeup and bathed frequently, but you couldn't tell based on the way guys inexplicably headed for the hills after just a date or two.

I was seventeen years old and I'd never even been kissed. Lots of other girls wouldn't have been able to say that if they'd gone on even just a couple of dates, but kissing some guy who was either going to turn invisible after the date, or who was going to take kissing as an invitation to do a whole lot more, wasn't really my style.

I probably should've made peace with the fact that this was just how my life was going to be, but I'd read entirely too many romance novels over the last few years to give up that easily on the idea of finding love. I just kept soldiering on, hoping that one of these times things would be different.

I didn't hold out a whole lot of hope though with regards to being able to fit in here in Clay, Wisconsin. I'd tried to keep a low profile at my last school, only to find out that whatever drove the nice guys to alternately chase after me and then run away once I started to return their interest still worked even when I wasn't making an effort to catch the eye of any of the guys in school.

If that pattern repeated itself again in a city as small as Clay, it would only take me a few weeks to run through all of the attractive guys in school, by which point all of the girls my age would hate my guts. Guys like that generally already had a girlfriend, whom they dumped along the way towards asking me out, with the result being that their ex-girlfriend, their ex-girlfriend's friends, and everyone else who'd ever wanted to date that particular guy treated me like a leper.

On the scale of really important things that people had to deal with, my problems were only a two or three, but that didn't stop me from wishing things could be different. The fact that my dad moved us around so often was both a blessing and a curse. On the one hand, moving meant that I would get at least a couple of weeks where everyone didn't hate my guts, which was a definite plus. On the other hand, moving around meant that I never got a chance to stay in one place for long enough to figure out if the girls at least would get over their dislike for me after a year or two.

I would've put up more of a fuss about being uprooted all of the time, but I knew how important it was to my dad to work his way up the professional ladder—that and I had an inescapable suspicion that it wouldn't matter how long I stayed, everyone would continue to hate me. Of course, that wouldn't have been much of a change from the way things were when we were always moving from city to city anyway, but if my dad hadn't gotten his current job five years ago and started this endless chain of moves, there was a chance that I would've lost my best friend Sally.

I'd known Sally my entire life. She was the most amazing girl ever, but I couldn't help but worry that our friendship wouldn't have survived if she'd been forced to watch one guy after another—some of whom she was interested in—throw themselves at me and then reverse course just as quickly on their way back out of my life.

If I had to pick between Sally and a dozen other girls, I would pick Sally every time. Besides, this way I never had to find out for sure whether it was possible for a group of girls to move past my strange curse once they'd seen it in action on somebody they'd been crushing on.

I parked my little blue Nissan and pulled out my phone so I could send Sally a quick text. She lived in Salt Lake City, Utah, so it was still early enough there that she hadn't made it to school yet, but not so early that I'd be waking her up.

Wish me luck. I'm about to enter the belly of the beast.

Good luck, sweetie. I hope that none of the boys in Wisconsin catch Dani-itis.

Her use of our personal shorthand made me smile. Dani-itis was what we called it when a guy threw himself at me and then lost interest after a date or two. My name was Danielle, but only my dad called me that. To Sally I'd been Dani since we'd entered grade school together.

Thanks, Sal. I'll keep my fingers crossed, but I'm not going to hold my breath this time. Any luck with your efforts to get Jesse to catch a case of Sally-not-itis?

Not yet, but I bought a cute new top that might do the trick. Even if it doesn't, buying it made me feel better.

Good luck—you'll have to send me pics after you're done doing your makeup.

It's a deal! All of my teachers are threatening to steal my phone if they catch me texting in class, though, so I'll have to wait until after school to update you on how things are going.

I throttled back a surge of self-pity and sent her back a smiley face before putting my phone away. I'd been hoping I'd be able to count on texting Sally to get me through my first day of school in a new place, but I couldn't begrudge her wanting to spend her lunch hour and her time between classes with her friends there. If anyone knew how hard it was to make and keep friends it was me, and I had a pretty good idea what it would do to her social life if she tried to be there for me every hour of every day.

I needed to just continue being glad that she was willing to spend so much time texting me when she didn't have something else going on. I couldn't imagine how much of a basket case I would be if I'd gone through the last several years without anybody to talk to.

I got out of my car and pulled my backpack out of the back seat as a single set of footsteps approached me from behind. There was no reason to think that anybody would be coming to see me, not given that I didn't know anybody here yet and the fact that there were already forty or fifty cars in the parking lot within a few dozen yards of me.

All of which explained my total surprise when someone slipped their arm around my waist and gave me a squeeze.

"Hello, new girl. Allow me to introduce myself. I'm Caine, Clay's official welcoming committee."

He got a tiny squeal of surprise out of me as I spun away from him. I was used to guys being forward, but not usually this forward—at least not this fast. Usually it took a day or two for even the most aggressive guys to decide they wanted to leave their girlfriend in an effort to catch me.

"Do you welcome all of the new students to school like that?"

"Nope, just the half that I've been assigned to take care of."

I looked him over as he responded to my question. He was tall, probably pushing six-two, with dark hair and smoldering blue eyes that were almost intense enough to stop me from noticing the way his gray polo shirt was straining to contain some of the largest shoulders I'd ever seen in real life.

Just based on how casually he touched me, I'd known that Caine wasn't going to end up being one of those shy, cute guys who lacked the confidence to actually make a move on a girl they were interested in. Still, I'd been hoping for somebody a little less devastatingly handsome.

He was hot enough that just having him talk to me was going to alienate a big chunk of the female students in my new school, but I just couldn't make myself be rude to him when he hadn't really done anything wrong yet.

"Let me guess, you're responsible for welcoming all the girls."

He smiled without taking his eyes off of me. "Smart as well as pretty. I knew this was going to be a good day."

I would've just blown his words off as the kind of insincere compliment I was used to guys using in an effort to impress me, but there was something in his eyes that was completely at odds with what he'd just said. I wasn't sure that I would have recognized what I was seeing if I hadn't just felt the exact same emotion seconds before. He was disappointed—before I'd even turned him down.

There probably weren't more than two or three straight girls in the entire state who would've felt relief at realizing a guy as hot as Caine wasn't interested in them, but that was exactly what I was feeling at that moment.

I'd arrived at Clay thinking that the best outcome I could hope for would be to find some guy who was confident enough to carry on a conversation with me, but not so confident as to act on the inevitable, inexplicable attraction that always followed. That particular combination of attributes was so rare as to be almost impossible, but it had happened one time three moves ago, and it was the first time since we'd left Salt Lake that I'd actually enjoyed going to school.

Even that situation hadn't been ideal. I'd known that Ben had wanted our friendship to turn into something romantic in nature, and that just by talking to him I was leading him on despite all of my efforts to keep things purely platonic between us. That knowledge had quite literally kept me up at night as I'd tried to balance my happiness against the potential unhappiness I might end up inflicting on Ben.

This, however, had the potential of being something much better even than that. If Caine really was disappointed in what he'd seen just now, then there was a good chance that he wasn't going to catch Dani-itis, which was unheard of in a guy who was confident enough to talk to me without any prompting on my end.

If I was reading the situation right, there was a chance that Caine could actually end up being a real friend, one who wasn't several thousand miles away, and whom I wasn't going to have to move away from in order to keep from causing problems in our friendship. I was ecstatic about the idea, so ecstatic in fact that I almost let him get away from me.

He'd already taken a step backwards by the time I realized that he was done being the 'welcoming committee.' I pinned him in place with a glare.

"What kind of welcoming committee swings by just long enough to feel up the new arrival and then leaves?"

Caine looked surprised that I was calling him on what he'd just done. "Ah, I have a class that I'm supposed to be getting to."

Normally I'm one of the least confrontational people in the world, but something about the situation was so weird that I just came right out and spoke my mind for once.

"Are you surprised that that bothered me? I saw you look at me and decide you weren't interested, which is cool, but weird. Even weirder is that you thought you'd be able to get away with that. What gives?"

Caine still looked off balance, but he managed a relatively nonchalant shrug. "Actually, I usually do get away with that. You're a very unusual girl..."

"Dani—Danielle, really, but everyone calls me Dani, which you would know if you really came over here to welcome me to the school."

"Right, Dani. Like I was saying, you're a very unusual girl."

I pretended to be getting mad. "Are you saying that any girl who doesn't immediately swoon for you is odd?"

Caine furrowed his brow as though weighing possible responses, and then shook his head in resignation. "Sure, let's go with that. I'm obviously devastatingly handsome, and you failed to react to my awesomeness, so that's as good of an explanation for what I was saying as any."

He looked so perplexed, which was obviously not an expression he was accustomed to wearing, that I couldn't help but laugh. "Good, I was kind of hoping you would say that, because it makes it a lot easier for me to say that you've got to be at least as odd as I am."

Caine arched one eyebrow. "This ought to be good. How exactly do you figure that I'm odd?"

I'd mostly been playing for time, but I was running out of things I could say that wouldn't come off sounding conceited, and I knew it. I debated half a dozen different responses before deciding that there was simply no way to salvage the situation.

"You know, it doesn't matter. If you can just point me to the office, I'll go get enrolled and head off to my first class."

I hitched my backpack up higher on my back and then turned to go, but Caine grabbed me gently by the arm.

"I would really like to know, Dani. I actually *am* very odd, so I won't hold anything you say against me."

The sincerity on his face was matched only by the feeling I got that he was once again concentrating very hard on something. I shook my head, fully intending on pulling my arm out of his grasp and walking away, but words tumbled out of my mouth as though of their own accord.

"Because you're the first attractive guy I've met in years who threw himself at me so quickly and then backed away less than two minutes later. You're not gay, are you?"

He snorted. "No, I definitely like girls. Look, don't get me wrong, you're very attractive, I just don't feel any overwhelming compulsion to pursue anything with you."

"I know, I could tell, which is awesome. That means you and I might have a chance of being friends."

"I take it that doesn't usually happen?"

The intense look of concentration was back on Caine's face. My instincts were screaming for me to pull back and pretend that I'd just been joking, but once again I found myself responding honestly.

"What the heck, it's not like we'll be here for more than a few months anyway. This is going to sound crazy, but guys throw themselves at me for a week or two and then all of a sudden lose interest for no reason at all. I don't know why it is—I'm obviously no Helen of Troy—but it's happened everywhere I've moved for the last several years. Once the guys do that, the girls all view me as competition and I walk around the school like some kind of ghost until my dad picks us up and moves to the next job. I think it's some kind of freaky curse or something."

I'd never been quite that honest with anyone about what was going on before then. I'd never told even Sally that I thought the endless parade of fickle guys was more than just an odd string of coincidences. It was surprising how much of a relief it was to just come right out and tell someone what was going on.

Caine cocked his head to one side and whistled. "You actually believe that, don't you?"

Now that I'd bared my soul that much, it was getting a lot easier to continue telling him the truth. "Yeah. If you don't believe me, just watch what happens over the next couple days. By the time the week's out at least two or three of the hottest guys in school will practically be getting into fist fights over me. You have no idea how relieved I am that whatever it is hasn't affected you like it does everyone else. I mean, what are the odds that the one guy my age in all of North America who isn't affected by this stupid curse would actually be here in the town I just moved into?"

"Are you sure you're not exaggerating at least a little bit? I'll bet I can find another guy in this school who won't try to sweep you off your feet."

The idea of potentially having not just one, but two guy friends was a heady thing. With just Caine not affected by my curse, I would have somebody to talk to, which would be amazing, but adding a second friend into the equation had the potential of changing things even more fundamentally.

If there was just one guy not catching Dani-itis, the rest of the girls in the school would still assume that I was some kind of man-stealing witch, but that I was just holding out for Caine. If there were two guys I was able to be friends with, then the girls in the school might correctly assume for once that the problem was with the boys who were going crazy rather than with me.

I gave Caine a considering look. "He has to be hot. I mean, my curse only seems to work on hot guys. The shy ones probably still like me, but they're just too scared to talk to me. You really think there's another guy as hot as you in this school who's not going to throw himself at me?"

Caine chuckled. "Well, in fairness, I'm not sure that there is anyone as hot as me in this entire state, but most of the girls in the school seem to think that Jerek is at least in the running for the title of most devastating guy in Clay, Wisconsin."

"Done. I will take that bet for any amount of money you want to name."

"My, you're hasty. You really should decide on the stakes before agreeing to the bet."

I shook my head. "You're probably right, but the truth is that I don't care what the stakes are if it means that I can avoid all of the usual drama that follows me around. Besides, I did stipulate money, which means that I don't have to worry about you asking for something else that I don't want to give."

"Well, you're lucky that I don't care much about money. I will take your bet, and find you another guy who is acceptably attractive, too competent for his own good, and who will most definitely not be throwing himself at you. When I win, you are going to come with me to every major convention—cheerleading or otherwise—I can find and help introduce me to as many women as humanly possible."

I looked at him suspiciously, but whatever weird planetary alignment had me more willing to bare my soul than normal still seemed to be in effect, and it was causing me to treat him like he hadn't just said something that made him sound like a complete stalker.

"You're paying, and it can't interrupt my schooling. My dad will never agree to let me miss school."

"That's it?"

"Not hardly. You're also going to have to get my dad to agree to these trips. That probably means a chaperone and a group that includes more than just the two of us. Also, these conventions have to be appropriate for a lady. I'm not going to lie to my dad about where we're going."

Caine's smile stretched from ear to ear. "Done. I agree to all of your terms. I know this is never going to happen, but we should agree what you win if somehow I don't manage to deliver on my promise. What do you want? Money? Fame? Special time alone with me?"

He moved his eyebrows suggestively and I found myself blushing. The truth was that I didn't have any idea what I wanted. Dad wasn't a millionaire or anything like that, but he was compensated very well for the analyst work he did, and the fact we moved around so much meant that the company covered stuff like our food, housing, and transportation.

When you got right down to it, I already had all the material things that I could reasonably ask for. All that was left was non-material things. I didn't particularly want to be famous—even assuming that Caine could deliver on something like that, which I found myself oddly sure he could. What I really wanted wasn't the kind of thing that anyone could guarantee me.

For my dad to work shorter hours, to be able to move back to Utah and spend time with Sally without it ruining our friendship, three or four friends here in Clay of both genders, or maybe just a stepmom who was so head over heels in love with my dad that she wouldn't mind the fact that her stepdaughter caused all of the available males in a ten-mile radius to behave like they were fourteen again.

None of what I wanted was particularly complex, but it was all completely unattainable and I knew it. Caine looked at me expectantly, and it almost seemed like I could feel some kind of pressure inside my head, pushing me to reveal the fondest desires of my heart, but this time I was able to push the urge off to one side.

"Let's go with money. They say it can't buy happiness, but it can't hurt."

"Smart girl. They're right, you know. Money can't buy happiness, but it can sure ward off a ton of unhappiness. One million dollars it is, to be delivered to whatever bank account you would like—offshore or otherwise—in a suitably un-traceable fashion. Now, let's get you over to the office so you can get registered."

I didn't actually believe he was going to deliver on his end of the bet—no random teenager had that kind of money to toss around—but that same weird pressure was back in my head, distracting me from challenging his assertion. By the time the discomfort subsided, the opportunity to protest his stakes had passed, and I decided to just let it go.

The next few hours flew by with unaccustomed speed. We walked into the building with me still unsure what to think of him, and that didn't change much between then and the end of the day.

I half expected him to drop me off at the office and then disappear, but instead he sat down with the guidance counselor and me and helped me pick my classes. In any normal world, no guidance counselor worth her salt would have agreed to have Caine in there with me, but Mrs. Spalding seemed to have zero issue with anything Caine wanted to do.

I was starting to believe that he hadn't been exaggerating when he'd implied that it was rare for him not to get what he wanted. Either whatever immunity I appeared to have was not as strong as I'd originally believed it to be, or he was just so charismatic that he was capable of bypassing my defenses with nothing more than his wit and charm.

However he managed it, by the end of our session with the counselor, I'd signed up for nearly every class he had at the exact same time that he had them. The one instance that wasn't the case was my substitution of a choir class in place of the gym class that he ended his day with.

I'd loved singing for as long as I could remember, but even so Caine nearly managed to convince me to forgo choir. If it had been anything less important to me he probably would've succeeded, but I held firm, and he shook his head as he walked me to my locker, which was, unsurprisingly, only two spots down from his.

"You're going to end up regretting choosing choir over PE, Dani, and then you'll have to beg me to come back down here with you and work my magic to get you out of all that dreadful caterwauling."

"We'll see. How exactly did you make that happen, and is it really going to stick? You heard Mrs. Spalding, if the teachers don't agree to sign me into the classes that are already full, then I'm going to be back down here tomorrow getting assigned a completely different schedule anyway."

Caine gave me a speculative look. "You're right. I don't need to convince you to drop choir, I just need to convince the teacher not to let you in."

I hit him in the arm, but not very hard, which was a good thing since his muscles were incredibly hard. If I'd actually tried to hurt him I probably would've broken my wrist.

"Ouch! Are you some kind of cyborg?"

"Serves you right. Maybe that will teach you not to hit people who've been nothing but nice to you."

I rolled my eyes at him. "Don't even start with me. You're not the wronged party here; you were threatening to take me away from my one and only love. Don't you dare keep me out of choir."

"I suppose I can let you add that as a condition to our bet—just this one time though. Don't start thinking that this is something I'm going to let you get away with on a regular basis."

"Don't think I didn't notice that you're dodging my question. Are you going to tell me how you work your magic?"

Caine put on an expression that was much too serious for him. "I very much doubt it. A magician never reveals his secrets."

I couldn't help myself, I laughed out loud as I followed him to our second hour class.

Chapter 2

Contrary to my expectations, Caine continued to escort me throughout the rest of the day. More than just escort me, he went out of his way to make sure that my first day wasn't as heinous as some of the first days I'd had over the last couple of years. It was so sweet the way he was trying to take care of me that I didn't have the heart to tell him it wasn't needed. I'd done this so many times that it took a lot to throw me off my game this early in the process.

It was what inevitably came later that gave me problems, but even that seemed like it was progressing more slowly than I'd come to expect. For the first time ever, I'd walked into a new school with a guy friend. Even better, this particular guy was intimidating enough that the rest of the guys in the school were thinking twice about throwing themselves at me. I could still see the wheels turning in the heads of a couple of the more confident, attractive guys, but even they spent a lot less time looking at me than I'd been expecting.

This was shaping up to be the best school since I'd left Utah, but I did find myself starting to second-guess my decision to enroll in choir instead of gym. Once I was out of sight of Caine, the guys started giving off more of the signals of early cases of Dani-itis than I'd seen anywhere else since I'd arrived. At least I knew this time I was second-guessing my decision for a reason other than Caine having turned on his charm to get what he wanted.

Predictably, the object of my thoughts was waiting for me at my locker after the last bell rang. "Admit it. You're starting to wish that you'd enrolled in PE."

"I don't have to admit anything of the kind. I'm a liberated woman. That means I'm perfectly able to say whatever I want."

This time it was Caine's turn to roll his eyes. "Whatever. I do have to say, though, that it's starting to look like my winning the bet is even more of a sure thing than I'd been thinking. To hear the way you were going on earlier, I half expected you to arrive here with a harem of five or six guys. What's going on? Are you losing your touch?"

I shushed him, looking around to make sure that nobody had overheard him. "Are you trying to make everyone hate me?"

"Hey, it's a fair question. My opportunity to meet tens of thousands of women rides on just how strong your little curse is."

I shook my head at him. "You're incorrigible. I'll have you know that this is all your fault. Normally stuff progresses faster than this—not as fast as you are implying, but faster. All I can figure is that you being around is interfering with the normal process. The other guys in the school must respect you a lot—that or they're completely terrified of you."

"Yes."

"That wasn't a yes or no question, Caine."

"Technically, it was an observation rather than a question, but even if it had been a question I still would've answered it that way."

I stuffed a handful of books into my backpack, but before I could sling it over my back Caine reached over and picked it up, shouldering it easily despite the loaded backpack already hanging from that same shoulder.

"So, how long exactly do we have to wait before your curse makes its presence known? A day? A week? A month? I just think we ought to establish some ground rules—you know, for the sake of the bet. I'd hate for you to try and rob me of my prize on a technicality."

I shut my locker and then shrugged as I led him past the office on our way out to the parking lot. "I don't know—not exactly. Like I said, this has never happened before, but I can't imagine you'll be dismissing my curse so readily two or three weeks from now."

"Hmm, sounds like I'd better plan for a month between when you meet my candidate and when you'll finally admit that I found a winner."

"Is it really so critical that you have an exact timeline?"

Caine looked at me with mock disbelief. "This is my future happiness we're talking about, Dani. There is a cheerleading convention in Atlanta in four weeks, and I can't afford to leave anything to chance. You're going to have to get your dad to let you go out to a party tomorrow night."

"I am?"

"Yes, if you don't meet Jerek tomorrow night I might not get a chance to introduce the two of you until next week."

Jerek. The name alone piqued my interest, but I did my best to keep my feelings off of my face. Caine had already demonstrated an industrial-sized gift at making me blush and I was resolved not to give him any more ammunition. "Who is Jerek, and why can't he have parties on the weekend like everyone else?"

Caine patted me on the cheek. "It's so cute the way you keep asking questions that you know I'm not going to answer."

"Seriously? You're not even going to tell me who this guy is?"

"Nope. I'm not warning him that I'm bringing you, and it just doesn't seem fair to give you that kind of an advantage."

I kind of wanted to stomp my foot and storm off—not because I was really all that angry, but because I was curious to see what he would do if I told him that the bet was off—but I didn't. Instead, I climbed into my car, accepted my backpack from him, and then drove off.

Forget about the million dollars, I wanted to see what would happen if there really were two guys out there my age who were immune to my curse.

My evening went about like I'd expected it to. I texted Sally to tell her about Caine—I didn't include any of the crazy stuff, just the fact that I'd met a guy who might be friend material—but her weak, almost indifferent, response bothered me a lot less than it would have if I'd still been thinking that she was the only friend I was ever going to have.

It was still too early to be getting excited about what Caine might represent, but I couldn't seem to help myself. The prospect of a friend, one who wouldn't get jealous of the attention I received from guys when my curse kicked in, was just too exciting.

On the home front, Dad had just started his new assignment in this area, which meant he was going to be working even later than normal. At the best of times I could look forward to pretty much the entire evening by myself, but when he first arrived in a new area and was trying to get a feel for the market so he could get started evaluating properties for purchase, it was rare for him to get home before I went to bed.

I'd long since stopped cooking meals for two—not that I'd ever been very good at it. I microwaved some food, ate dinner, worked on my homework, and then watched some TV before it was time to go to sleep.

Ever since Mom had died, I'd been considered the morning person in our family, but given the kind of hours my dad normally kept that wasn't saying much. It usually took a couple of iterations of the snooze button before I managed to get myself out of bed, but I woke up the next morning five minutes before my alarm even went off and flew through my normal morning routine.

I made it to the school almost twenty minutes before the first bell was due to ring. To my surprise, Caine was waiting in the parking lot for me, sitting on the hood of some muscle car that had been done up in pinstripes and a massive blower that I was pretty sure hadn't come standard from the factory.

"Oh, my, Dani, you really are anxious to meet Jerek."

I made as if to punch him in the arm again and then remembered just how solidly he was built. I pulled the blow at the last second.

"I'm not going to this party unless you tell me more about what I'm getting into. Seriously, what kind of guy throws parties on a school night?"

Caine raised one eyebrow and I felt a familiar sense of pressure in the back of my head, but I just gritted my teeth and refused to back down. After several seconds he shrugged.

"You really are odd, Dani."

"Most people don't consider that to be a compliment, Caine."

"Most people don't have my advantages in life." He made as if to get up and walk towards the school, but I grabbed hold of his arm and latched on. Caine looked expectantly at his arm as though waiting for me to let go, but when I refused to release him he finally answered me.

"Okay, Jerek stays busy on the weekends, so that leaves weeknights as the only available time to party."

I cocked my head to one side. "Most people who like partying so much that they'll do it on a school night tend to stay busy on the week-end *by* partying, Caine."

I'd said the words slowly, as though talking to a small child. Most people would have taken offense at my tone, but Caine just chuckled. "You've got a point there, blondie. Jerek isn't like most people, though. He doesn't actually like partying, so you're not headed off to some kind of depraved den of drugs and alcohol. Trust me, as parties go, this one is going to be pretty tame."

"I don't get it. If he doesn't like parties, then why is he throwing one tonight?"

"Believe it or not, the parties are his parents' idea."

"Oh, I see. His parents are the depraved party animals."

Caine rolled his eyes at me. "Yeah, not so much. They are just...concerned...about his lack of a social life. They're kind of worried that he's never going to find a girl and settle down."

The pressure had disappeared for a minute or so there as Caine had been telling me about Jerek, but it was back now, and I felt an almost overpowering urge to drop my line of questioning. I shot him a dirty look.

"I can feel you doing whatever it is you're doing. People aren't just pawns for you to move around however you'd like."

"Actually, they are. Not pawns, but very susceptible to...suggestion. I try to only use it when it's in their best interest, but there you have it. People pretty much give me whatever I want—not you, though. Do you have any idea how fascinating that makes you?"

"I believe the term you just got done using was odd."

"Are you going to hold that against me?"

"I don't know. It probably depends on how hard you push." Even as the words left my mouth, I realized that I should be a lot more worried about whatever it was Caine was doing to me. Things had been so new yesterday that I hadn't fully realized the pressure I'd been feeling was him trying to force his will on me, but now that I sort of understood what was going on, it seemed like the kind of thing that should be making me worried.

"Are you stopping me from freaking out?"

"A little, but not as much as I normally would have to in this kind of situation. At the risk of you thinking that I'm calling you weird again, would you be willing to share why it is that your natural instinct isn't to go running off into the hills yelling at the top of your lungs?"

The urge to tell him what he wanted was back, but this time my frown was accompanied by a very stern stomp of my right foot.

"I'm serious, Caine. If you keep doing that the bet is off and I will never talk to you again."

He held up his hands in an 'I surrender' gesture and a moment later the pressure inside my head vanished, even the low-level influence that he'd been using to keep me calm. I examined my feelings and found that he was right. I didn't really want to run away from him.

It was hard to say for sure if it was simple curiosity keeping me there, or if it was the crushing loneliness I'd been dealing with ever since I'd left Utah. Either way, part of me knew staying around someone who could influence my decisions like this probably wasn't the smartest thing I could be doing, but I just couldn't seem to work up any kind of real concern regarding Caine's intentions.

I was still debating what to say, but apparently we'd made it to the end of Caine's patience. "You do realize that if you don't reward my good behavior, I'm much more likely to go back to being bad, right?"

"It feels like I'm being manipulated into giving you what you want no matter what."

"It probably feels that way because that's exactly what's going on. Now are you going to tell me or what?"

I took a deep breath and gave him a serious look. "Do you promise that you're not trying to take advantage of me somehow, and that you'll stop trying to push me into doing things against my will?"

Caine looked at me for several seconds and I got the feeling that I'd just asked for something much weightier than I'd realized. The silence between us stretched out for so long that I'd almost given up on getting an answer out of him by the time he finally nodded.

"I promise. No more funny business."

His words weren't all that remarkable in and of themselves, but there was something about the way he said them that told me in his own way Caine was just as lonely as I was. That, more than anything else, decided me.

"Okay. I guess it comes down to the fact that not all guys head for the hills after the initial attraction wears off. The worst kind of guys are affected differently by my curse. They come after me like they're not going to take no for an answer. I've learned to pick them out pretty early on in the process and find a way to avoid them at all costs. It's a really big bummer to find out a guy you thought was a pretty decent sort actually thinks that date rape might be an acceptable means to an end."

Caine's usual lighthearted mien had vanished even before I'd started talking, but now he looked every bit as serious as I could've hoped. "I'm sorry, Dani. That has to be hard."

"Yeah, sometimes it makes it hard to see the good in people, but really I'm fortunate when you get right down to it. I've got a built-in creep detector. Once you get over the disappointment of knowing what people are like on the inside, it's actually one of the few upsides to my curse.

"You don't need to be sorry though. So far you're not registering on my creep detector even a little bit. I guess that counts for even more than I'd realized. You may be plenty weird in your own way, but I honestly don't think that you want anything bad to happen to me—or anyone, really."

Caine bowed, a curiously graceful gesture that looked like he'd practiced it at some point in the not-too-distant past. "Your virtue—and your secrets—are safe with me."

Caine offered me his arm and then escorted me into the building as though intent on warning off any guys unwilling to take no for an answer.

The rest of the day blew by at warp speed. Sharing classes with Caine was every bit as fun as I'd thought it would be. There wasn't a serious bone in his body, but by the same stretch his joking wasn't mean.

It shouldn't have come as a surprise that our teachers let Caine get away with a ridiculous amount of shenanigans. Under other circumstances I might've been irked that he was so determined to lighten the mood inside of our classes, but it turned out to be exactly what I needed. It was telling that he hadn't been quite as much of a goof-off the day before. Apparently, he'd been able to tell that I needed a less serious environment after our heart-to-heart that morning.

The guys in my classes were starting to get a little more aggressive than they had been the day before, and I could see the wheels starting to turn in Caine's head as he got his first taste of seeing my curse in action. I'd known that something like this was inevitable—the real surprise was that everyone was still significantly behind where I would've expected them to be under other circumstances.

Given that the boys hadn't started throwing themselves at me yet, it pretty much went without saying that the girls hadn't all united against me yet, but it was worth noting that more than one girl gave me an envious look at the way I was able to interact so freely with Caine.

It was yet another bit of evidence that Caine really was a pretty stand-up kind of guy. Based on the amount of effort it had seemed to take for him to use his mystical powers of persuasion on me, I was pretty sure it wasn't the kind of thing he could casually use on large groups of people. That meant he could put the whammy on any one girl, but there was no way he was putting the whammy on everyone enough to make them overlook jerky behavior if that was the norm for him.

All in all, it was a pretty good day right up until I went into my choir class. A couple of heartbeats before the bell rang, a guy and a girl I'd seen holding hands the day before slipped into the room, but this time they obviously weren't happy with each other.

The girl, a very pretty redhead with flawless skin and the kind of long, straight hair that always made me jealous, had obviously been crying. The guy, a tall blond who was sporting a surfer look, just looked annoyed, but I didn't think much of it until we were released to start warming up our vocal cords.

I turned to one of the girls sitting next to me, intending on asking her if we could run the exercises together, but the surfer guy grabbed my elbow before I could get any words out.

"Hey, my name's Peter. Do you want to warm up together?"

I felt my smile freeze onto my face. I'd been so stupid. Under normal circumstances, I would have remembered to talk to one of the girls next to me even before class started to avoid giving someone an opportunity to corner me like that, but having Caine around for so much of the day had made me sloppy.

I turned back to the girl I'd been planning on approaching just seconds before, but she'd already paired off with someone else. "I…ah…I suppose that would be okay, Peter."

I didn't give him my name, even though I knew not doing so was rude, but that didn't seem to deter him at all. I started humming the first exercise, but Peter only made a token attempt at joining in.

"So, you just moved in yesterday, right? What's your name?"

"Everyone calls me Dani. It's nice to meet you, Peter, but I would really like to get warmed up. This is my favorite class all day and I don't want to miss anything."

Peter nodded. I could tell he wanted me to think he was listening to me, but it was obvious he was focused on his next line. "I totally get that. This is one of my favorite classes too. Listen, a bunch of us are going to get together tonight for a party on the lake. I was thinking it would be fun for us to go together. What do you say?"

A range of possible responses started through my mind, everything from just telling him to get lost to turning him down politely, but there wasn't anything new there that I hadn't tried a hundred times already. Rude had never been my style though, so this time I tried just being honest.

"Peter, who was that girl who came into the class with you today?"

"Oh, that's Tamara. I wouldn't say we came into class together, more like we just happened to walk through the door at the same time, you know?"

"So...you're not with her? I know I'm new here, but it seemed like you guys were a couple yesterday when I was watching you."

Peter still had that look on his face, but this time it seemed to be saying that he'd focused on the bit of my response that had included me watching him. That wasn't particularly helpful, but I told myself it wasn't fair to be thinking overly harsh things about him at this point.

It had become pretty apparent over the last few years that guys didn't have a lot of control where my curse was concerned. If he got past the initial attraction and turned out to be the kind of guy who refused to take no for an answer, then I could feel free calling him whatever dirty names seemed appropriate inside the privacy of my own thoughts, but until then I needed to give him the benefit of the doubt.

"I'm going to be completely honest with you, Dani. Tamara and I have been going out for a while, but we're not together anymore. I haven't been feeling it for a little while now, so I broke things off today. It's always hard on both parties to end a relationship, but I've always felt like it's important not to drag things out once you know they aren't working out. Really, I was thinking of Tamara when I did it. I don't want to string her along and make her feel like there's a future if it's not going to work for both of us."

My smile had gotten even more strained, but I just kept repeating my mantra of giving Peter at least a little credit. Maybe if I handled the situation just right, I could make him see the craziness of what he was doing. It had never worked before now, but there was a first time for everything.

"How long had the two of you been dating?"

Peter was finally starting to look uncomfortable. I figured that had to be a good sign.

"A year—maybe a year and a half."

"And how long would you say that you haven't been 'feeling things' exactly?"

"I don't know, a while. Look, if you don't mind, I would really rather not talk about Tamara. I'm really broken up about everything that's happened, but I think going to this party will be a good way to get my mind off of what I'm feeling right now."

Despite my mantra, Peter slipped a couple of notches further down on the decent guy scale. He wasn't broken up about anything, and I knew very well that his doubts about his relationship with Tamara had probably started about fifteen minutes after he'd seen me come into choir for the first time the day before.

"Look, Peter, I'm sure you're a nice guy." Normally. "But I just don't think that would be a good idea. I have other plans tonight, but even if I didn't, I still wouldn't be interested in going out with you."

Judging by the sudden change in his expression, Peter was finally listening to me rather than just trying to catch enough of my responses to adjust his approach. Saying that he was unhappy would've been as big of an understatement as I knew how to make, and for a brief moment I thought maybe he was going to turn out to be one of those guys who was willing to go to any lengths to get what he wanted, but after several moments of obvious inner conflict, he just nodded and went back to his position in the tenor section.

I knew I hadn't seen the last of Peter, and I had the sinking sensation that I was entering uncharted waters with regards to how he was going to respond once he'd had time to think about my rejection. It was like there was some kind of cosmic scale that someone was monitoring in order to make sure that I didn't have too much good come into my life without an offsetting amount of terrible coming along for the ride. Caine had the potential of being my first new friend in years—my first guy friend ever—so of course I'd completely screwed up my initial exchange with one of the most confident and aggressive guys in the entire city of Clay. Sometimes it just seemed like I couldn't catch a break.

Our teacher, Mr. Benton, looked ready to start practicing, but then his cell phone went off and he stepped into his office, leaving everyone free to go back to talking. I was half afraid that Peter would come back for a second attempt, but instead the brunette to the right of me gave me a measuring glance.

"I'm not sure what you were trying to accomplish just now, but if you're really not interested in Peter, you should come right out and say so. Tamara is a really nice person and she doesn't deserve what he just did to her."

I shrugged helplessly. "I thought that's what I just did. I don't know how else to get that message across to Peter without just being rude."

"I don't know what to tell you, but he doesn't look like a guy who was just shot down, he looks like someone who's gearing up to take another run at you."

I wanted to argue with her, wanted to tell her that any normal guy would back off after being told point blank that I didn't want to date him, but I knew it wouldn't do any good to open my mouth. I was right. Under normal circumstances, a brush-off like that would be plenty severe enough to crush the hopes of the vast majority of guys, but my curse was anything but normal. I looked over at Peter and he smiled at me in a way that left no doubt as to the fact that, to him, my rejection had sounded an awful lot like 'please try harder.'

This Jerek guy Caine was taking me to see had better turn out to be the real deal. At the rate things were going, I was going to need another platonic guy friend if I was going to survive the three to six months I was going to be stuck in Clay.

Chapter 3

Caine carried my books from my locker to my car again after school and then entered my phone number and address into his phone before closing my door and tapping the roof of my car.

"I'll be by your house to pick you up in half an hour—don't forget to bring your swimming suit."

If there's one thing designed to make a girl break the speed limit, it's being told that she only has half an hour in which to get ready for a surprise swim party. Given that I was a new arrival in Clay, and I was surprisingly worried about what both Caine and Jerek thought of me, I didn't just break the speed limit, I shattered it.

Luckily I made it home without getting pulled over and changed—in record time—into the black bikini I'd picked out at the beginning of the summer, which left plenty of time to examine my appearance in the full-length mirror in my bathroom. Caine had said to bring my swimming suit, but I was not about to change out of my clothes while standing behind a couple of trees in the middle of nowhere. Besides, it's always a heck of a lot safer to try on the swimming suit before you let people see you in it. My clothes weren't feeling any tighter than normal, but that wasn't any guarantee that I hadn't put on an extra pound or two that were going to be disgustingly obvious once I was wearing a few bits of fabric that were thin enough they could easily be pulled through a wedding band.

Once I'd reassured myself that I didn't need to go looking for one of my old one-piece suits, I slipped on some board shorts and a baby T. I actually felt like I looked pretty good, but it was hard to say for sure. I could snap a picture and send it to Sally, but best friends basically have to tell you that you look good no matter what. It was amazing how devastating having guys fall all over you could be when you knew it was just because of some metaphysical feedback loop that was going to send them packing just as fast as they'd shown up.

Luckily I didn't have very long in which to second-guess myself. Less than a minute after I finished pulling on my clothes Caine called my phone to announce that he was waiting for me downstairs.

I slid my phone and a twenty-dollar bill into my jacket pocket as I hurried toward the front door. Caine gave me a jaunty wave from the driver's seat as he fiddled with his stereo. I shook my head at him as I opened up the passenger door.

"You know it's considered polite to get out of your car and knock on my door, right?"

"Sure, but I wouldn't want to freak you out and make you think your curse was starting to work on me. Besides, my rakish disregard of societal conventions is a big part of my charm. Ready to meet the second hottest guy in the country?"

I would've rolled my eyes at him, but I was too busy trying to keep the butterflies in my stomach from flying up my throat. It was crazy; I knew next to nothing about this Jerek guy, and I would've been disappointed if he threw himself at me like Peter had just done, but I couldn't deny the fact that some part of me wanted exactly that—just not because of my curse. I wanted a guy to pursue me on my terms.

"Are you really not going to tell me anything about this Jerek guy?"

"Nope, like I said, it just doesn't seem fair."

Normally I'm not really a violent person, but the urge to hit Caine in the arm again was almost overpowering. It really was too bad that he wasn't slightly less muscular. I was going to have to see if it made a difference if I hit him when he wasn't expecting it, but I had a sneaking suspicion that it wouldn't.

"What about the party? Will you at least tell me where we're going? My dad's pretty relaxed about what I do during the day, but I didn't tell him I was going anywhere and if I'm not back by the time he gets home, I really will be grounded until I'm old enough to go to college."

Caine suddenly looked concerned. "What time will your dad be back? I forget that normal people have things like curfews."

"What? Your parents seriously don't care when you get home?"

"Not really. It's hard to get too worked up about that kind of thing from six feet under the ground."

I suddenly felt like the most insensitive lump in the entire world. "I'm so sorry, Caine, I never should've said—"

He waved away my apology with his characteristic nonchalance. "You don't need to be sorry. It happened a long time ago and you had no way of knowing. Really, I barely think about them anymore. I've been on my own for so long that this feels like the natural state of affairs."

"How did it happen? I mean, if you don't want to talk about it, that's fine, but if you need to talk about it with somebody, I'm here for you."

Caine looked at the clock on his dashboard and then shook his head. "It's okay. I would relate all the gory details to you, but it's really not that big of a deal and we don't have very long before we'll be arriving at the boat. As much as I would like to keep you completely in the dark regarding all things Jerek, I suppose I should probably tell you where we're going—once you can confirm what time I need to have you back home to Father dearest."

I didn't get the sense that Caine was lying exactly, but for the first time I could remember I felt like he was keeping something important from me. I considered pressing him on it, but that was a pretty insensitive thing to do given that we were talking about his dead parents. Besides, I still felt an almost overpowering urge to trust him, and there was no sign that he was using his mystical powers of persuasion on me.

"I'm pretty safe counting on him not getting back until eleven. Honestly, I wouldn't expect him home before midnight, but it's almost guaranteed that if we stay out till then, this will be the one night he comes home at ten and starts freaking out over the fact that I'm not there waiting for him."

"Awesome. I can totally have you back before then. Jerek shuts his parties down promptly at nine-thirty so there's plenty of time to get everyone back to the mainland by ten."

I shook my head in astonishment. "Seriously? What kind of guy stops a party at nine-thirty? Wait, you said mainland?"

Caine nodded. "Did I not tell you to bring a swimming suit?"

"Yes, but where I'm from, wearing a swimming suit does not automatically mean that we're going into a body of water big enough that getting out of it constitutes 'going back to the mainland.'"

Caine shrugged. "I guess I should've been more specific. Around here, if someone tells you to bring a suit, you can pretty much bank on that meaning that you're headed up to Lake Superior."

"So what, we're going to some kind of island?"

"Bingo. Jerek's parents have a summer house on Madeline Island. It's the only one of the Apostle Islands that's not part of a park or a national forest or something. As for your other question, Jerek doesn't like to be up late on school nights, and since it's his place—or his parents' place at least—we kind of have to abide by his rules."

My head was spinning. "So...I guess he takes his schooling seriously then?"

Caine laughed so hard he practically choked. "Yeah, that's not the reason. Jerek gets all of his homework done every day, but he shows up in class for a grand total of about forty minutes, just long enough for him to get the next day's assignment and hand in what he did the night before."

"Oh. I have to say I'm a little disappointed."

"Oh, no, Dani, are you trying to tell me you have a thing for geeks?"

"Not really—don't get me wrong, I like geeks about as much as I like any other kind of guy—you just got my hopes up there for a minute because I thought you had a friend who was a nerd. You almost blew my whole mental image of you."

Caine took his eyes off of the road long enough to roll them at me and then gestured at a parking lot off to our right. "Very funny."

"I certainly thought so."

"That's good, because making fun of poor little old me cost you your last chance to ask me another question about the party. We're here, and you're out of time."

I stuck my tongue out at him and then turned to take in my surroundings. 'Here' turned out to be a parking lot almost as big as the one at the school, a parking lot that led down to a set of boat ramps on one side and a full-blown marina on the other.

I looked across the water and was struck by just how big it was. Dad had never taken me to the ocean, which meant the biggest body of water I'd ever seen before this had been the Great Salt Lake. It went without saying that Lake Superior was enormous, but the characteristic that stood out to me the most was the fact that it wasn't as dead as the Great Salt Lake.

There are plenty of pockets of green in Utah, but I'd never seen anything there like the massive green canopy staring back at me as I looked along the parts of the shore that were visible from where Caine had parked. I'd come expecting something very much like experiences that I'd already had, but judging on just what I'd seen so far, I was in for quite the shock.

Caine closed his door and walked around to where I was standing with my body pressed between the car and the door. I caught him chuckling again as he gently pulled me out to where he could close the door.

"Come on, there's nothing to be worried about. The Loch Ness monster is on the other side of the world."

As quickly as Caine had showed up at my house, I'd expected for us to be the first ones to arrive, which had been just fine with me. To be honest, I would've preferred to meet Jerek in a setting other than a party. Even before my curse had popped up I'd been uneasy in big crowds, but I'd been mentally gearing up for exactly that given that Caine had been clear this was going to be a party.

Despite my attempts to prepare myself, I wasn't ready for the riot of color and movement waiting down by the water. Apparently when Jerek complied with his mother's orders he did so in a very big way. This wasn't a small undertaking, it was a group of teenagers that had to number at least thirty. Apparently word of the party had spread quickly while we'd been in school.

I slowly followed Caine over to one of the boat ramps, where a blond guy our age was nudging a large motorboat off of the trailer that he'd backed into the water. Unlike the rest of the onlookers, Caine didn't wait to be asked for help. He handed me his phone, wallet and keys and then stepped out into the water to help the blond guy guide the boat off of the trailer.

I took the opportunity to study the guy Caine was helping, who presumably was Jerek. With some names I already had a mental image in my head of what someone was going to look like just based on someone else I'd met with the same name. I'd never met a Jerek before this though, so I hadn't known what to expect before I laid eyes on him for the first time.

'Wow' didn't even begin to cover it. He was tall—at least six-two—and his hair color was the same as Peter's, but that was where the resemblance ended.

Jerek had shoulders that were even broader than Caine's, and he had the muscles to go with them. I caught a hint of gray eyes as he looked back towards the big SUV pulling the trailer, and I felt my heart skip a couple of beats. I'd always liked gray eyes and blond hair, and the fact that his hair was wavy without looking messy just made him even more attractive.

If I'd stopped there and not taken in everything else, I would've said he looked like some wholesome, all-American quarterback, but there was a lot more to Jerek than that. He had a piercing on the right side of his lower lip—a simple ring—and a complex set of tribal symbols running up and down both of his arms.

Jerek looked like exactly the kind of guy that my dad didn't want me meeting. Generally speaking, I tried very hard to be obedient to my father. I figured he was the one earning the money that kept us from starving, and he was a lot more experienced so it didn't hurt to listen when he had advice or concerns, but there was just something about Jerek that made all of the concerns I knew my dad would have fly right out the window.

Jerek and Caine got the boat maneuvered the rest of the way off of the trailer, and then Caine steadied it, standing chest-deep in the water while Jerek climbed in and turned on the motor.

"Can you park the rig for me, man?"

Caine nodded like the two of them had done this so often that it was a well-practiced routine. As he waded out of the water I found myself walking over to the passenger door of Jerek's SUV. I suddenly didn't want to be standing there by myself, surrounded by all those guys from school, while Caine parked the trailer.

Caine gave me an inquiring look as I climbed into the vehicle with him, but didn't say anything about my sudden bout of cowardice. We parked the SUV, and then walked back over to the dock where everyone else had gathered.

Looking at the mass of people who were waiting for Jerek to bring the boat around, I figured there was no way we were going to make it into the first boatload of people. The way that

Caine dragged his feet as we got to the floating dock seemed like confirmation of that fact—right until Caine took a deep breath and then grabbed my hand to pull me onto the dock.

His anxiety when it came to stepping onto the moving wooden platforms became understandable as the first dock moved violently in response to our weight. I'd been on amusement park rides that were less heart-stopping, and I found myself wondering how the marina had let their docks get in such a bad state of repair. I hadn't watched the rest of our classmates clamber out to the end of the dock, but based on what we experienced just in the first few platforms we crossed, it must have been quite the trip.

"Are you going to be okay, Caine?"

I got a nod in response, but he didn't say anything, which finally made me realize that Caine was still holding his breath. It was my turn to give him an incredulous look, but he didn't stop to explain and I found myself gingerly stepping from dock to dock as he plowed on ahead, navigating the treacherous movements with care.

Apparently we were quite the spectacle. The kids from our school actually tore themselves away from watching Jerek guide the boat in so that they could watch us. I'd never seen Caine so out of sorts. Usually he was never happier than when he had an audience, but this time he was so focused on his footing that he didn't even seem to realize anyone was watching until we made it out to the second-to-last platform at about the same time that Jerek's boat bumped up against the dock.

The docks had already been sitting a little low on the water from the weight of so many bodies, but Caine and I were the proverbial straw that broke the camel's back. As soon as we stepped on the dock containing the back half of the partygoers, the wood dropped down low enough that water splashed over the top of my feet for a moment.

That drew gasps out of our classmates, which seemed to snap Caine out of his funk. He looked from one person to the next, spending several seconds on each of them as Jerek started helping people into the boat. It took me a few seconds to realize that Caine had dusted off his mystical powers of persuasion, but more surprising was that Jerek seemed to be doing the same thing to each person as he helped them board his watercraft.

The revelation that the two of them were using their abilities to wipe the memories of everyone present was so shocking that I would've stopped in the middle of our section of the dock and stared dumbly at Jerek except for the fact that Caine didn't give me a chance. He had hold of my arm and kept me moving forward.

"Come on, Dani, Jerek's holding the last couple of spots open for us."

"I'm not sure I want to get in the boat anymore."

Caine looked away from the dock that had been his primary focus once he started moving forward again and frowned at me.

"Nothing is going to happen to you, we're just making sure that a new round of rumors doesn't start at school tomorrow."

"I'm not imagining it then, am I? You really are making the dock move like you're some kind of sumo wrestler? It's not just the fact that the dock is old and needs to be rebuilt, is it?"

The two of us were close enough, and I was freaked out enough by what was going on, that I'd talked in something that was only barely more than a whisper, but Caine still flinched and looked around at the rest of the kids from our school like he was expecting one of them to suddenly start screaming that he and Jerek were aliens.

"This isn't the time or place for that particular discussion, Dani. Besides, you already knew I wasn't just another regular guy. Why is this freaking you out so much?"

I felt the barest hint of pressure starting inside my skull, but it stopped as soon as I shot Caine a dirty look. "I told you not to do that to me."

"Sorry, force of habit. Usually when something like this happens, that's my go-to response. Look, I'm the same guy who hasn't been triggering your creep-dar. Will you please get in the boat? I promise I'll explain as much as I can about what's going on once the two of us have a chance to sit down together in private."

I gave him a suspicious look, but he was right. He still wasn't tripping any of the internal alarms I used to decide whether or not someone was dangerous. After a couple of seconds I sighed and worked my way between our classmates so that I could climb into the boat.

Jerek helped me into the boat just like he had the rest of our classmates, but not without trying to play with my memory the same way he had everyone else's. This time the sense of pressure didn't just build gradually, it went from being absent to full force, and it was much stronger than anything Caine had ever used on me. Either Caine had been taking it easy on me, or Jerek was in a league all his own. I was inclined to think it was the latter.

Everyone else he'd used his powers of persuasion on had looked a little confused for a second right after his ability took hold. Even after they'd recovered, it had still seemed like they were mentally off somewhere else. I could've faked the same response and just let him think that he'd succeeded in making me forget the way the dock had wobbled all over the place as Caine had walked out to the boat, but I was feeling oddly confrontational.

Instead of going glassy-eyed and smiling at him, I met his eyes and gave him a challenging look. He'd already started to let go of my hand by that point, but my response caused him to do a double-take.

Apparently he wasn't used to anyone being able to resist him. Caine cleared his throat from behind me and I realized he was waiting for the two of us to get out of the way so he could get into the boat.

Given the way I was feeling at that moment, if he'd been anyone else I would've been tempted to tell him to climb around me, but I really didn't want him capsizing the boat, so I allowed Jerek to pull me over to the far side of the boat so we could serve as a counterbalance as Caine climbed across the gunwales.

Jerek waited until Caine had pushed off from the dock, and then brought the boat's motor up to the point where it started us chugging along towards the markers that signaled it was okay for boats to move at full speed. He looked at me again and then back at Caine.

"You didn't tell me you were bringing someone. Did you know she was so…unique?"

"Yeah. I thought about telling you, but I figured if I did that you would've canceled the party. I didn't want to miss out on the fun of seeing your face when you realized what you are up against."

I half expected Jerek to give Caine the dressing-down he seemed to think that his friend needed, but he just frowned again and returned his focus to driving the boat.

I'd been left standing awkwardly between Caine and Jerek, completely unsure of what I was supposed to do next. Moving to the front of the boat and sitting on one of the benches would've been tempting if not for all of the guys already sitting in the circular seating arrangement that seemed to be so common in the front of boats like this.

There were an equal number of girls scattered throughout the group—all of whom looked attractive and fun—but I knew from past experience that their presence wouldn't stop things from getting awkward. A bunch of the guys in the front of the boat had their backs to me, and some of the ones who could see me still looked like they hadn't fully recovered from whatever Jerek had done to them, but the two who seemed to be the most with it mentally looked like they were starting to reassess their choice in female companionship, which was the last thing I wanted.

Caine came to my rescue with his usual perceptiveness, pulling me back against him in a possessive manner as we hit the calm water markers and Jerek pushed the throttle forward. The boat shot away with such incredible acceleration that I probably would've gone over the side if Caine hadn't tightened his grip around my waist. I didn't know how Jerek could've seen that, at least not well enough out of the corner of his eye to have registered what was going on, but he frowned and I got the feeling that it was in response to Caine's arm around me.

I was starting to wonder if my bet with Caine was going to end up being worth it. Finding a second guy who was capable of resisting my curse wasn't especially useful if he turned out to be a complete jerk.

Despite my misgivings, it was too late to do anything about my situation unless I was prepared to jump out of the boat while it was moving at high speed and swim back to the shore—which I wasn't. I was just going to have to ride it out and see what happened.

I decided to focus on our surroundings to take my mind off of all of the unpleasant things that might happen before the night was over, and that proved to be a good choice. The lake hadn't gotten any less beautiful as we left the marina behind and started towards the big island I could see off in the distance.

Given that it was the only one of the chain of islands here that was subject to private ownership, I'd half expected Madeline Island to be so full of houses and roads that there wouldn't be any room for actual vegetation, but that wasn't the case at all. As we got closer I could make out a number of houses—some of them monstrously big—along the shore, but other than a small space around each of the habitations, the greenery was just as thick on Madeline Island as it was on the others that

Caine had indicated were some kind of state or national park.

I knew it might very well be a carefully crafted illusion, that we might arrive and find that the trees and underbrush were only a few yards deep, but for now I was happy to believe that Madeline Island was exactly the kind of garden paradise that Caine had made it sound like.

We made really good time, which was a testament to just how fast Jerek's boat was. It only took a couple of minutes before we were slowing down so that we could pull up next to a dock that belonged to the single largest house I could see on that side of the island. Caine had made it sound like Jerek's parents were rich—you pretty much had to be wealthy in order to have a summer house—but I'd been expecting something much smaller. You could have dropped each of the last six houses my dad and I had lived in over the last few years into Jerek's summer home and still not have managed to fill it up.

The outside was a combination of smooth stones and massive windows that could've felt jarring given that people had favored much smaller windows back when they'd originally been building with rock like that, but which just ended up complementing each other in ways that I wouldn't have anticipated.

From our vantage point down low on the water, it was hard to see everything, but I was pretty sure there was a swimming pool and a massive hot tub up at the top of the steps that led down to the dock where a second boat was moored. It seemed a little silly to have a swimming pool when there was a lake less than eighty yards from the back door, but if you had money to burn and wanted to be able to swim during the winter, it probably made sense to put in your own private pool.

The clear glass enclosure at one end of the pool looked like it was capable of being rolled out to cover up the entire pool area, which seemed to validate my suspicions. Jerek's parents had built the house fully intending on being able to go out for a dip regardless of how cold it might get during the winter, which blew my mind. It was hard to believe anyone would be willing to pay to have that big of a body of water heated year-round through the bitter Wisconsin winters. Their electricity bill must be roughly the price of a small car every month.

I was still shaking my head in amazement as Jerek cut the engine and let the boat drift the rest of the way up to the dock. Caine let go of me and hopped out of the boat with the smoothness that was a clear signal that Jerek's parents had made sure that this particular dock wasn't going to tip over regardless of how much weight was put on it.

Caine helped me out of the boat, and then reached down to assist a tall brunette who'd queued up after me. She flashed an inviting smile at him before heading down the dock towards the stairs up to the house, and I wondered if I should be doing the same thing, but I didn't particularly want to leave Caine's side.

That turned out to be a mistake. Caine was halfway done helping people out of the boat before I realized that one of the guys who'd been sitting in the front of the boat with his back to me was none other than Peter. I looked around, hoping against hope that he'd patched things up with Tamara, but there was no sign of her and my stomach dropped as Peter gave me an angry look.

"I thought you said you had other plans when I invited you to this party."

Caine jumped in before I could come up with a response. "She did, Jenkins, she'd already agreed to come here with me. Now are you going to be cool, or is Jerek going to ferry your butt back to the mainland when he goes back there to pick up the second load of people?"

A trickle of people had continued past Caine as he'd faced off with Peter, which meant that the boat emptied out while Peter was still trying to decide the best way to respond to Caine's challenge. The seconds stretched out to a point a hundred miles past uncomfortable, and then Jerek stepped between the two of them.

"Correction. The question is whether you're going to leave the lady alone, or if *Caine* is going to ferry you back to the mainland."

Caine didn't look particularly happy about the idea of playing chauffeur, but before he could get a word in edgewise Jerek poked him in the center of his chest.

"I told you I didn't want to have a party this week, and not only did you tell everyone that I was having one anyway, you brought along an unexpected surprise. You can either spend half an hour playing taxi driver, or I can tell my mother that it's time for you to take a trip over to Africa."

Caine winced, but to his credit, he didn't back down immediately. Everyone but Peter had already made their way off of the dock and up the stairs leading to the house, and it took only a heartbeat's effort for Caine to make Peter's eyes go fuzzy in a clear indication that he wasn't going to remember what was being said.

Caine ordered Peter to climb up onto the dock and go to the house, and then once he was satisfied Peter was going to carry out his instructions, he turned back to Jerek. "Look, I'm sorry if I overstepped my bounds, but it's a really bad idea to leave Dani alone with Peter, or pretty much any other guy here."

Jerek shrugged. "You have a choice. You can either leave her here under my protection, or you can take her with you in the boat, but if that means you have to make an extra trip to ferry over everyone who's waiting back in the marina, you'll just have to make the extra trip and hope you don't miss out on all the fun."

Caine sighed and climbed back into the boat before turning around with his hand outstretched to me. "I'm sorry, Dani. I didn't expect things to go down quite like this. I would say that Jerek's not usually this much of a jerk, but he keeps telling me I need to stop lying so much."

I started to move towards Caine, but there was something holding me back. Despite the fact that he was giving Caine such a bad time, Jerek so far hadn't set off any of my internal alarms. Despite his rough exterior, he wasn't actually dangerous.

When you added in the fact that he had so far shown even less of a reaction towards me and my ever-present curse than Caine had, Jerek would've been an enigma even without the vibe I'd gotten from him as I started moving back toward the boat. There was no way for me to know what either guy was actually feeling at that moment, but I got a strong impression that Jerek didn't want me to get back into the boat with Caine. He wanted me to stay. In fact, I was pretty sure he was making Caine drive the boat at least partly as a way of splitting the two of us up.

It was an odd play out of someone who'd otherwise shown almost zero response to my presence, and it made me even more intrigued by the blond-haired bad boy who seemed to be trying so hard to pretend that he couldn't care less about me.

I turned back to Caine and prayed that he was both as trustworthy as he seemed and a decent judge of character. "I don't want you to miss out on any more of the party than you have to. If you think I'm safe here with Jerek then I'll stay so you can get as many people in the boat as possible."

Caine studied me for several seconds as though trying to divine the actual intent behind my words, and then sighed. "Jerek is the most trustworthy guy I know. If he says that he'll keep you safe and not let Peter or any of the other guys hassle you, then that's exactly what he'll do."

I nodded and turned back to Jerek. "It looks like I'm with you for the next little while."

Caine cut back in before Jerek could respond. "I want your word, Jerek. You don't leave her alone and you don't let anything happen to her. Dani is special in ways I don't completely understand yet, but one thing I know is that guys will throw themselves at her if you or I aren't there to warn them off. Do you promise?"

"You have my word, Caine. No harm will befall her while I still breathe. Does that satisfy you?"

"No, but if it's good enough for Dani, then it's good enough for me."

Caine reached over the gunwales of the boat and pushed off of the dock before turning the motor back on and driving away. A minute later it was just Jerek and I standing alone on the docks. Jerek looked at me for several seconds as though not sure what to do with me now that I was there, and then turned and started towards the stairs.

"Wait, where are we going?"

"Up to make sure that nobody has started destroying my home. My mother wants me to socialize, but that doesn't mean that she'll be happy if she returns here to find that someone's gotten drunk and set one wing of the house on fire."

"I thought Caine said that there wasn't going to be any drinking at this party."

Jerek didn't look back to make sure I was keeping up, which seemed like a rather poor way to make sure that I was going to be taken care of while he had responsibility for me.

"Caine says a lot of things which bear only passing resemblance to reality. The truth is that I work very hard to keep these gatherings under control, but even I can't stop this many people from getting into a certain amount of trouble. I'm sure that at least two or three people snuck vodka over in their water bottles. Once they become inebriated enough for it to become noticeable I will inform them that they're no longer welcome here, but unless you want me to have Caine spend the rest of the afternoon ferrying drunken louts back to the mainland, we'll both have to put up with the presence of people with whom we don't particularly want to associate."

I was pretty certain that was a thinly veiled reference to the fact that Jerek wished he didn't have to spend time with me, which was all the more confusing given the vibe I'd been picking up from him earlier. Was it possible for someone to not want me to leave and yet still wish they didn't have to be around me?

We arrived at the top of the stairs and I looked around to see that the pool area was every bit as posh as I'd thought it was. The biggest difference now was that there were nearly a dozen high-school kids splashing back and forth between the pool and hot tub.

The pained expression on Jerek's face was so contrary to the image I had of him as a tattooed and pierced bad boy it was almost funny, but I wasn't particularly tempted to laugh at him. Caine never seemed to take himself too seriously, but Jerek was another matter entirely. I got the impression Jerek wasn't the kind of guy who forgave perceived insults easily.

Once Jerek was satisfied that nobody had yet gotten so drunk as to be in danger of drowning, he headed into the house without looking back to see if I was following him, which was actually a fairly safe bet. Between my desire not to be left alone with Peter, or any of the other guys who were probably gearing up to hit on me as soon as Jerek was out of earshot, and my eagerness to see the inside of his mansion, there was no way I was going to let him leave me behind.

I should've known that Jerek would find a way to suck the fun out of even an experience as amazing as seeing how the top one percent of the top one percent lived.

Saying that his house was breathtaking didn't even begin to do it justice. We walked through halls paneled in a dark wood that I knew had to be expensive simply because I'd never seen anything like it before. The furniture was all leather, and as we passed through a quick succession of rooms, I saw such a bewildering array of different shapes and sizes, I finally realized yet another way in which the ultra-rich were different than the rest of us. I'd grown up thinking that furniture was no more complicated than a couch, easy chair, desk chair and the chairs that we used around the table in the kitchen, but Jerek's family had a whole different standard when it came to furnishing their home.

It was like each selection had been carefully handcrafted by an array of artists working from a common vision, and the results were making me dizzy. My favorite was a triangular-looking concoction that looked like a cross between a loveseat and a sofa. The top was only just wide enough for two people to sit next to each other while the bottom flared out so that whoever was sitting there could spread their legs as wide as they would go and still not bump into the other person's feet.

We passed rooms with gorgeous white carpet that was so lush I wouldn't have dared step onto it while wearing my shoes, and I couldn't help but shake my head at how casually Jerek treated his surroundings.

"I can't believe you let people from our school come here without way more supervision than this."

Jerek shrugged. "It's not my call. My mom said that she wants me to have at least weekly parties out here, so I make it happen."

"Isn't she worried about someone trashing your place? I sure would be."

Something unidentifiable flickered behind Jerek's eyes, but once again it was gone so quickly that I almost could've believed that I'd imagined it.

"Some things are more important than possessions or money. Making sure that we do our part for society, and keeping in mind the greater good, is more important than any of that." He spoke with the air of someone who was repeating a party line that he didn't particularly believe in. "My mother believes so completely in the preeminence of her cause that she feels no sacrifice is too great in the pursuit of her goals."

"But you don't?"

Jerek suddenly looked tired. "I don't know. Six years ago I would've told you that I believed exactly the same thing as my parents. Their goals were my goals and no sacrifice was unreasonable if it brought me closer to realizing the destiny I thought was laid out before me."

I was almost scared to open my mouth for fear that doing so would cause him to remember how much he disliked me, but I was too curious to let an opportunity like this pass me by.

"What happened?"

"I saw the world in a different way, one that didn't gel completely with everything I'd been taught growing up. Pure certainty like my mother has rarely survives contact with reality, at least it didn't for me."

Jerek shook himself as though realizing that he had said more than he'd intended, and I realized that my chance to find out more about him had passed. I was more disappointed by that than I'd expected to be. I'd come here hoping to find a friend, quickly been convinced that Jerek could never be that individual, and then only minutes later come to realize that there was a lot more depth to him than I would've expected out of someone who grew up surrounded by the kind of luxury on display around me.

I knew it was probably a mistake to push him for more this early in our relationship, but I couldn't help myself. I opened my mouth to ask a probing question about what he believed in now, but he'd already started up a set of stairs in order to confirm that all of the interior doors to areas he didn't want his guests visiting were locked.

It was time to change strategies. "Does someone else live here with you? I mean, I'm just wondering how the doors would've ended up getting unlocked since the last time you were here."

"No, nobody else lives here. I don't even live here for most of the week, but we have a cleaning crew that comes through several times each week and they occasionally hire a new person who doesn't understand the importance of locking up as they leave each section of the house."

I'd been hoping for more than that. If Jerek had had a brother or sister living in the house with him, then I could've asked about them, but there weren't a lot of places I could go when it came to questions about his cleaning company—at least not places that would tell me more about who Jerek really was.

I followed him in silence as he checked nearly a dozen additional doors, before coming up with another question that felt like the right blend of personal and nonthreatening.

"So where do you stay when you're not out here on the island?"

"I've got a smaller place in town where I spend a lot of my time. It doesn't make sense to come all the way out here during the week when I have to go to school every day. The commute just isn't worth it."

I had about a dozen questions regarding his 'smaller' place in town, but before I could move on to them, I realized I had a much more pressing concern.

"Would it be okay if I used one of your bathrooms?"

"Sure, there are a couple downstairs. I'll take you there once I'm done checking out the third floor."

Apparently I'd been even more enthralled with trying to figure Jerek out than I'd realized, because I was suddenly certain I wasn't going to make it another twenty minutes while he finished checking all of the doors.

"I'm really sorry to be a bother, but is there any way we could go to the bathroom sooner than that—like, maybe right now?"

Jerek gave me the kind of look you give a three-year-old when they tell you that they have to go potty five minutes into a long car drive despite having proclaimed repeatedly before getting in the car that they didn't need to use the bathroom. I half expected him to give me directions and tell me to go find the bathroom by myself, but after a single long-suffering sigh he pulled out a set of keys that fit a door that he'd just confirmed was locked.

"You can use the one in here."

'In here' turned out to be the single largest bedroom I'd ever seen. I started to follow Jerek through the door until I saw what looked like another acre of the same soft white carpet that had been so prominent downstairs. There wasn't any reason to think that I had anything on the bottom of my shoes, but I could only imagine how embarrassed I would be if I tracked mud into such a pristine area.

Jerek had turned around in the center of the room so he could see me and was looking in my direction expectantly. A more confident girl would have simply walked across the carpet and assumed that everything would be okay, but I pulled off my flip-flops before leaving the hall and just hoped that he wouldn't think I was too much of a spaz.

I started across the carpet towards Jerek and practically swooned at the sensation of the soft carpet against my bare feet. The feeling was so pleasant that I made it nearly all the way to Jerek before I came back to myself enough to register the rest of my surroundings.

The room we were in was obviously a bedroom—the massive bed that dominated the wall off to my right would have settled any question there—but other than the bed, it was surprisingly unlike any bedroom I'd ever been in before. The far wall was taken up by more than a dozen large floor-to-ceiling windows and a set of French doors that opened onto a balcony that was bigger than my room back home, but that wasn't the really odd part.

As I turned and looked back toward my shoes I saw that the wall closest to the door was dominated by an array of weapons that would've looked much more at home in a martial arts dojo or a castle armory than inside a bedroom belonging to one of the richest people on the planet. Massive two-handed swords shared the wall with hammers that were as tall as I was and a variety of other edged and blunt instruments of destruction filled up the wall in a display of deadly metal like nothing I'd ever seen before. I cast about for an explanation of what I was seeing, but unless Jerek's family was getting ready to film some kind of beat-'em-up action flick, there wasn't any easy answer for the presence of so many weapons in what appeared to be a functional place to sleep.

"So do you guys collect weapons as a hobby?"

Jerek scowled. "Look, do you need to use the bathroom or not? I didn't bring you into my bedroom so we could play another round of Twenty Questions, and I really would like to get the rest of the house secured before someone gets into something that they're not supposed to."

The intensity of his response would've taken me aback all by itself, but if anything I was more unnerved by the fact that it was Jerek's bedroom we were standing inside. When you got right down to it, it was silly to feel uncomfortable being alone in a room together with a guy my age, but that didn't change how I felt. Based on some of the looks I'd seen directed Jerek's way on the way here, most of his female guests would have given just about anything to be in my position, but I wasn't like them.

My curse meant that I'd never been able to spend alone time with any guy before I met Caine, and regardless of where he and I might end up in the future, right now the two of us were worlds away from spending time in his bedroom, or mine. I might be a modern girl living well after the time when being alone with someone of the opposite gender resulted in a shotgun wedding, but the truth was that I'd lived a pretty sequestered life that—in this area at least—had a lot more in common with that of my grandmother than it did with the experiences normal for someone my age.

That meant that everything else about the situation felt all the more heightened. The fact that I wasn't wearing any shoes shouldn't have made any kind of difference in my level of uneasiness. It wasn't like flip-flops actually covered up much, even assuming it had been a big deal for someone to see my naked feet, but the simple fact that I'd taken off part of my original attire had fist-sized butterflies bouncing around inside my stomach.

My board shorts and baby T weren't particularly daring attire compared to the string bikinis a lot of the other girls were wearing, but I was suddenly conscious of just how much of my legs were showing. It was one thing to fantasize about meeting a guy who was immune to my curse and spending some alone time with him, it was quite another to find myself having skipped several of the steps in my normal dream script.

I could feel myself blushing, but I tried to blow it off as being the result of anger at the tone he'd taken with me. "No need to get so snippy. I was just trying to make polite conversation. If you'll point me to the bathroom, I'll go do my thing and get out of your hair. Assuming that you trust me to lock up behind myself, you don't even have to wait for me if you don't want to. It's obvious that I've already been far too much of a burden on you. I'll just go find a quiet spot so that I'm out of your way. If I stay quiet enough, maybe there'll even be a chance that none of the guys downstairs will find me. It's not a great chance, but I'd rather deal with that than deal with you."

The girl I wanted to be, the one who was confident enough to tell off somebody like Jerek, would've stared daggers at him the entire time she was talking, but I wasn't that girl, and I really needed to pee. Instead, I spun in place looking for the bathroom door.

There were only two doors inside the room, so I figured I had a fifty-fifty chance and just picked one. I figured it was a good sign that Jerek didn't start laughing at me as I headed away from him, but I still breathed a sigh of relief as I pulled the door open and saw a massive white bathroom waiting for me on the other side. I slipped inside and locked the door before he could say anything.

Predictably, the bathroom was just as stunning as the rest of the house, but even that couldn't distract me from the urge to start sobbing. I managed to hold things together until I was in front of the sink washing my hands, but even as tears started running down my cheeks, I refused to make any noise. I wasn't going to let Jerek know that he'd gotten to me like that.

Meeting Caine couldn't be the start of an entirely new life for me. Whatever it was that made guys behave like idiots when they saw me was just a fact of life, and I needed to resign myself to that.

I dried my hands on a towel that felt like someone had managed to weave it out of clouds, and shook my head at my stupidity. Even as I told myself that I was going to stop hoping for a different lot in life, I knew it wasn't true. It didn't matter what I told myself, it would just be a day or two before I would be back to wishing that things could've gone differently with Jerek.

I just couldn't figure him out, and that bothered me as much as anything. He was ridiculously rich, and yet his room was full of old weapons rather than tens of thousands of dollars of high-end electronics. His house was roughly the size of a football field, but he drove a thirty-thousand-dollar SUV instead of a two-million-dollar supercar. He'd been incredibly mean to me, but Caine seemed to think that he wasn't as big of a waste of time as my first impression would've indicated.

Not only that, he wasn't anywhere near as shallow as I'd been expecting out of someone who threw weekly parties that included dozens of girls who doubtlessly threw themselves at him every chance they got. His story about how he'd come to adopt a different belief system than his mother hinted at a depth that I'd rarely encountered in anyone, let alone someone with his kind of advantages in life. Usually, depth like that went hand-in-hand with suffering, and so far I hadn't seen much indication that Jerek had ever had any occasion to experience real suffering.

I hadn't come to the party hoping Jerek would end up being my boyfriend, I'd just come hoping he would turn out to be a friend. It was possible to survive without a guy—millions of women did exactly that every single day—but I wasn't so sure it was possible to survive without any friends at all. I pulled out my phone and debated calling Sally, but I just couldn't bring myself to do it.

The odds were good that if I called she would answer the phone and tell me all the things I needed to hear, but I just couldn't quiet the voice inside my head that told me I would be imposing on her by taking her away from her Utah friends—her real friends. Besides, I could hear Jerek shifting around his room and knew that he'd decided I wasn't trustworthy enough to be left there unattended.

That didn't stop him from being a jerk, but it was his house and regardless of how rude he'd been to me, I wasn't going to descend to his level. I was going to be polite—even if it killed me. I blotted my tears away with a tissue and then walked over and unlocked the bathroom door.

I tried to edge past him, but Jerek casually blocked my way. "I'm sorry about that, Dani. You didn't deserve that, and even if you had, it would've been rude of me to treat you like that. The truth is I hate these parties more than almost anything. I'm not up here checking the doors because I'm worried about the cleaning crew having left doors unlocked, I'm up here because this is one of the few valid excuses I can provide when my mother asks why I didn't spend more time down with my guests."

"I don't understand, Jerek. If you really hate these parties so much, why do you throw them? Tell your mom that you're not going to do them anymore, or failing that, just tell her that you're throwing them but don't actually invite anyone."

Jerek shook his head. "I wish things were that easy, but they aren't. My mother is unbelievably good at knowing when someone is lying to her. I've done something that I can't ever afford to have her find out about, and the only way to keep it a secret is to play these games with her. As long as she's focused on the parties and me going to school, she's too busy to realize that she's fighting the wrong battles."

"Why are you telling me this? I mean, I'm glad that you are, but I guess it just seems really out of character."

Jerek stepped back out of my way as though giving me permission to leave, but I no longer had any urge to storm out of the room. I'd come here wanting a friend, but I was realizing even that wasn't as alluring as understanding what drove Jerek.

"There are a lot of reasons that I'm telling you, Dani. I was unconscionably rude to you, you who of all people deserve better than that."

"You already said that."

Somehow I'd crossed most of the distance between us without realizing it. It was almost as though my curse had decided to start working in reverse, but I knew that was ludicrous. I would've blamed it on whatever mystical powers of persuasion Jerek and Caine both seemed to possess, but there was no telltale sense of pressure inside my head.

My heart was pounding away in my chest as though it was about to spontaneously combust, and I felt like an idiot to be considering kissing a guy I'd known for less than an hour, but the urge was nearly overpowering and Jerek didn't seem to be backing away from me.

"I know I already mentioned that reason, isn't it enough?"

"Not if there are others. Why me of all people? Why not Caine or one of the girls downstairs who are desperately wishing they could throw themselves at you right about now?"

We were only inches apart, not quite touching despite the fact that I desperately ached to have him take me in his arms, and I was starting to have a hard time focusing on his words.

"I think that I'm telling you this because I'm tired of pretending to be someone I'm not. When I set out on this course I had no idea how hard it was going to be. I knew it would be hard, but I didn't have the frame of reference to understand that there were things a million times more difficult than anything I'd ever dealt with before."

I reached down and took his right hand in mine. For most people it would've been a small gesture, but for me it was like running the world's first three-minute mile. It was beyond huge, and I kept expecting him to pull away from me, but he didn't.

"I'm sorry, Jerek, I don't understand what you're going through, but I'm willing to listen if it will help."

His hand was warm and seemed to be sending little tingles of electricity up my arm. I looked up at him and desperately wanted him to kiss me. For a moment I thought he was going to do it. He leaned forward as though just as hungry for me as I was for him, but then at the last moment he shook his head and pulled back.

"It's happening faster than I thought it would, Dani. It's not safe for us to be together like this. Come on, I'll get you downstairs. You can wait for Caine on the dock and I'll stand at the top of the stairs to make sure none of the guys from school hassle you."

I felt like he'd reached into my chest and ripped my heart free of my body. If someone had asked me when I'd woken up that morning if I was ready to be kissed for the first time, I would've told them that there was no way under the sun that was going to happen, but somehow Jerek had changed all of that. He'd slipped through my defenses like they weren't there, only to change his mind after I'd all but thrown myself at him.

I started shaking, as if the emotions I was feeling were simply too powerful to be contained inside of my body. Jerek reached out as though intending on comforting me, but before I could decide if I was willing to be comforted by him after he'd rejected me such a short time before, he changed his mind and pulled his hand back close to his side.

"I'm really sorry, Dani. If there was any way for things to be different I would take it, but there isn't. You need to get downstairs for your own sake, and I need to stop touching you for mine. Trust me when I say it's for the best."

I shook my head at him. "None of this even makes any sense. Are you using that thing you and Caine do on me? Are you making me want you? I can't feel it this time—unlike every other time the two of you have tried to force me into doing something against my will—but it's the only explanation for why I would be feeling this way."

Jerek drew back as though I'd struck him and then turned and walked out of the room, pausing only long enough to drop one last bomb.

"Yes, Dani. It's not happening the way you think it's happening, but this is my fault. I'm the one who's doing this to you, and if you don't leave and never come back, your life as you know it will cease to exist."

Chapter 4

I couldn't think of a response I was less prepared for than the one I'd just received, but Jerek was already fifteen feet down the hall and showing no signs of stopping to wait for me to catch up. I hurried out of his room, stopping only long enough to lock his bedroom door and pick my flip-flops up, but despite my speed, he was already out of sight—presumably halfway down the stairs by then.

This was the first time I could ever remember chasing after a guy instead of being chased, but that didn't stop me from doing exactly that. I ran down the stairs with reckless speed and still didn't manage to gain more than a foot or two on him. He was almost to the front door, which meant my chance of getting an answer out of him—at least an answer that had a chance of being the truth—was just about to vanish.

He wasn't going to want to bare his soul to me out in the middle of the pool party any more than I would've wanted to bare my soul to him under similar circumstances.

"Jerek, wait. Please wait."

I thought he was going to ignore me. We were more likely to have privacy here inside his house than we were out by the pool, but even that wasn't guaranteed. It was entirely possible that one of our classmates was lurking just around the corner hoping to overhear some kind of juicy gossip, which was all the more reason for Jerek to blow me off.

His hand was on the doorknob, but for some reason my words made him pause, and I only needed a couple of seconds to catch up to him.

"I'm sorry. I didn't mean to push too hard or ask the wrong questions. I'm just having a really hard time trying to figure you out. Is there any possible way for us to go back to how things were before?"

If it had looked earlier like I'd hit him, now a distant observer would've been entirely justified in thinking that I'd just stabbed him with one of the weapons from inside his bedroom. Jerek was facing me, hand still poised to open the door, but he was looking down at the ground as though unable to bring himself to face me. I was even pretty sure that his eyes were closed.

I went back over my words looking for something that could explain his reaction, but I came up blank. I opened my mouth to apologize again—this time intending on keeping my mouth from running on about wanting things to be different, but he finally looked up at me with tortured eyes.

"No, Dani. Despite what you or I might wish, things can never go back to how they were. Not for you and me."

He pulled the door open and started to exit the house, only to stop with his nostrils flaring. I turned, intending on finding out what it was that had caused him to pull up so abruptly, and my entire world stopped making sense.

For a split second everything out in the pool area looked normal. There were just over a dozen guys and girls scattered around the edge of the pool and sitting in the hot tub, but none of them were moving. That was the first thing I noticed as I stepped forward close enough to touch Jerek.

They were still breathing, and their eyes were open, but nobody's mouth was moving.

I was scanning the hundred-and-eighty-degree arc visible from where I was standing in an attempt to figure out what was going on when I first saw it. At first I thought it was one of Jerek's guests. It was bigger than any of the people I remembered riding over on the boat with us—bigger even than Caine or Jerek—but it had two arms, two legs, and a head so my mistake wasn't entirely unreasonable.

Generally speaking, I felt like I had no room throwing stones at pale people. My curse meant that I didn't spend a lot of time at places like beaches or swimming pools, so getting a tan had always seemed fairly pointless—especially considering the whole bit where it increased my chances of skin cancer.

There were plenty of actresses these days with really flawless skin who didn't go for the whole over-tanned look, but the...creature that caught my eyes wasn't anything at all like that. It was white, but it was a sickly, unnatural white—like one of those fish that lived hundreds of feet underneath the surface of the ocean, or something that had spent thousands of years inside of a cave.

That probably should've been my first real clue that the thing I'd spotted wasn't one of our classmates, but it wasn't until it turned and looked at me that I realized just how much danger we were all in. A pair of small, piggish eyes were set above a mouth that was too elongated to have ever been descended from the same genetic stock that had spawned my distant ancestors, but it was the claws that were the most disturbing. They were more than a foot long, and obviously had never been intended for anything other than rending flesh.

For one impossibly long second, the creature stared at Jerek and me without moving, and I thought my heart was going to stop. The sense of pressure building in my chest was nothing less than crushing. I wanted to say that I'd never experienced anything even remotely similar, but even as I had that thought I knew it wasn't true. The sensation of pressure had started in my chest, but it had already sent tendrils up into the base of my skull and there was a second epicenter of pain blossoming in my skull only an inch or two below the spot where I felt pressure when Jerek or Caine tried to compel me to do something.

The similarities were more than just disturbing—especially in light of how odd Jerek had been ever since I'd arrived at his home—but I forced myself to focus on the differences in the hopes that those differences meant that Jerek and Caine weren't any kind of close relation to whatever kind of creature was slowly moving towards Jerek and me. I wanted to scream in the hopes that someone would come save us, but Jerek reached back and squeezed my hand reassuringly.

I would have asked him what was going on, but at that precise moment I could feel him inside of my mind using his ability to try to force me to remain silent. He wasn't any more able to force me to do something I didn't want to do now than he'd been a few minutes earlier, and I was very aware that there was still a chance he was somehow in league with the creature headed our way, but despite everything that had happened so far, I still had a strong urge to trust him.

The creature was closer now, close enough that I was pretty sure it could cover the distance between us and attack before I could do anything to get out of the way, but Jerek still had a hold of my hand. I took a surprising amount of solace in that simple contact, screened as it was behind his body so the creature couldn't see it. The creature opened its mouth, revealing vicious-looking pointed teeth and a forked tongue, right before it sprang at us.

Only it never made it to me because Jerek let go of my hand and intercepted it several feet short of its destination.

I would've said that no individual, no matter how fast or strong, could've stood against the monster that seemed intent on eating me, but somehow Jerek was doing exactly that. He stepped into the creature and punched it in the stomach with enough force to pick it up and throw it backwards through the air nearly a dozen feet.

It was an awe-inspiring attack, but even as Jerek's punch connected with the creature's stomach, the creature's claws raked him across the back. I'd been able to see light from the setting sun reflecting off of the edges of the creature's natural weaponry as it had stalked towards us, and I had no doubt but that those claws were razor-sharp, which meant that despite Jerek having landed the initial blow, he'd just sustained a mortal injury.

Only he hadn't.

It went against everything I'd learned up until that point in my life, but those unnaturally sharp claws didn't cut into Jerek's unprotected flesh, they skipped off of his back like a sword that had just been slammed into solid rock.

The creature sailed through the air and collided with a tree on the far side of the pool area, and then things got even weirder. Jerek and the creature both had moved with impressive speed in their initial exchange of blows, but as soon as the creature rolled to its feet, they both started moving so fast that I wasn't able to really follow the fight anymore.

I initially thought it was just because they'd decided to pull out all the stops in their attempts to kill each other, but as the seconds passed I realized that didn't fit with what I was seeing. A light breeze had kicked up since Jerek and I had gone inside his house, but the trees weren't just gently swaying back and forth, they were moving in fits and starts like what you saw when watching someone dance to a strobe light.

I blinked in an attempt to force my eyes to start working again, but that didn't change anything and the breeze didn't feel right on my skin anymore. It now felt like I was being assaulted with erratic puffs of air that were coming at me at the same time that the ambient sounds around me cut in and out.

I tried to move—wanting to help Jerek despite the fact that I had no idea how to fight something that was capable of cutting me in half without even trying—but none of my limbs were moving like they should've been and I fell to the ground in an odd, jerky fashion as though time was skipping forward without bringing me along for the ride.

I hit the ground hard enough to sprain my left wrist, but I hardly even noticed because I was so caught up in watching Jerek and the creature fight. I couldn't have said for sure based on how much of the fight I seemed to be missing, but it didn't seem like either of them was busting out any kind of fancy martial arts moves. They just waded into each other like a pair of old-fashioned boxers intent on battering each other into submission.

Jerek connected with blow after blow and most of them looked like there was enough force behind them to snap my neck if I'd been on the receiving end, but the creature was possessed of an unnatural vitality that allowed it to get back up time and time again despite the punishment it was receiving.

Jerek was just enough faster than his opponent that he was able to avoid most of the blows that the creature aimed his way, and the few that got through bounced off in exactly the same fashion that the first attack had. I would've said that the fight was completely mismatched given the beating that the creature was receiving and the fact that it'd so far been unable to mark Jerek, but there was something about Jerek's manner that told me he wasn't just toying with the creature. This fight was for real, and he seemed very much convinced that one wrong move could get him killed despite whatever preternatural defenses had carried him through up until that point.

Despite my best efforts, I blinked and the creature seemed to teleport from the far end of the pool area where Jerek had driven him all the way over to my side of the yard. I looked up at its inhuman black eyes and was convinced I was a goner, but Jerek was only half a step behind the monster, and he slammed a punch into its ribs with enough force that I heard them crack in the instant before the creature spun around and stabbed him in the stomach with its claws.

By that point Jerek's shirt was little more than scraps of fabric hanging around his neck, so I was able to see the claws start to skip off of the hard planes of the stomach for a fraction of a second before his flesh gave way. The creature tried to rip its claws laterally through Jerek's flesh, but he was too quick for it.

He trapped its wrist with his right hand and then slammed his left fist into the creature's elbow with enough force to snap its arm. I half expected the creature to shrug that off like it had everything else up until that point, but apparently a broken bone was a broken bone even for it.

The creature tried to tag Jerek with its other hand, but he pulled its claws free of his stomach and then ducked the blow before landing a powerful uppercut to its chin, snapping its neck.

The pressure inside my chest disappeared even before the creature hit the ground, and I knew it was dead, but my relief was short-lived. Jerek grabbed my hand even as he pressed his left arm against the wound in his stomach, and started pulling me towards the dock as his head whipped back and forth in an attempt to watch every direction simultaneously.

"Come on, we've got to get to the water right now."

I let him pull me along, but I was too shocked to process everything that was going on.

"I don't understand what just happened, Jerek. What about everyone else?"

He didn't slow in the slightest at the reminder that there were a dozen other people who'd been as helpless as babies before the creature's compulsion, but I could see him breathing deeply as though trying to sample all of the scents in the air.

"I can't save everyone else. I'm not even sure I can save you and me. Now hurry or else we're never going to make it out of here if there are more hunters in the area."

"Wait, you mean there are more of them? How is this even possible?"

Jerek pulled even harder on my arm, and I felt him reaching into my mind and pushing in an effort to get me to snap out of it and start moving at something more than a fast walk.

"I don't have time to explain right now, Dani. You're just going to have to trust me. It's vitally important we get out of here right now."

Once again, I could've tried to resist his compulsion, but it was a lot easier—and a lot smarter—to just go along with it, and I found myself running along behind him as we got to the top of the stairs leading down to the dock.

"Can't you fight off the others if they show up? I don't want to leave everyone else here."

"No, I can't fight off any more of them today. The poison on the first one's claws has already worn down most of my natural resistance to its attacks. If I go up against another one, it's going to cut me to ribbons before I manage to put it down."

We got to the end of the stairs before I could ask any more questions, and Jerek lifted me into the boat as he kicked the metal attachment points that were holding the boat against the dock. It shouldn't have surprised me after everything else I'd seen in the last few minutes, but I still did a double-take as the metal fasteners ripped completely free of the wooden dock rather than breaking every bone in his foot.

The motor on the boat turned over on the first try, and Jerek instantly threw the throttle all of the way forward as he cut the wheel hard to the right. We passed within inches of a large rock, but I got the feeling that this wasn't the first time Jerek had zipped away from the dock at full speed.

The boat we'd ridden over from the mainland had been breathtakingly fast, but it had nothing on the one we were in now. We seemed to fly across the water, and rather than being exhilarating, it just added to my fear. I looked around for a life jacket. I was pretty sure that there had to be some on the boat, but there weren't any out where I could see them, and I wasn't about to relax the death grip I had on my seat to go start rummaging through the compartments up towards the front of the boat.

I had a million questions that I wanted to ask Jerek, but I wasn't sure I wanted to distract him while we were moving at what felt like ninety miles an hour. Instead I just focused on the front of the boat and tried not to notice the way the water was whipping past us, or how hard we seemed to hit every time the boat cut through a wave.

That meant I was completely unprepared when Jerek swore. "You're going to have to pull yourself together, Dani."

"Seriously? You haven't told me anything. How am I supposed to pull myself together when I don't even know what's going on?"

Jerek pointed towards the mainland. "There are two more of them up there, and it looks like Caine doesn't have much longer. I need you to drive."

"What? No, I can't drive this thing. My wrist hurts and even if it didn't, I don't know the first thing about boats. I thought you said you couldn't survive fighting another one of them."

"I probably can't, but I don't have any other choice. Those things are between us and my vehicle. Besides, I'm not going to just leave Caine to die."

"So you won't leave Caine, but it's fine to leave all those other people back there?"

I couldn't have said where those particular words came from. Normally I wasn't anywhere near that confrontational, but apparently I was even more shaken by my entire world being thrown on its ear than I'd realized. Jerek scowled at me and grabbed my arm, pulling me free of my seat despite everything I could do to hold onto it.

"You don't have a choice about this, Dani. You'll either drive this boat, or you'll explode in a massive ball of fire when it hits the shore. Your call, but you only have a couple more seconds in which I'll be around. After that you'll be on your own without any clue what you're doing."

As he spoke, Jerek angled the boat to the left, which made absolutely no sense to me given that it had us headed to a point a hundred yards to the left of Caine and the hunters I was finally able to see now that we were several seconds closer. Jerek cut the wheel hard to the right as he pulled me into the seat he'd just vacated, and then he put my right hand on the throttle.

"Forward is fast, pulling it back towards you will slow you down, but remember that you don't have any brakes. The water's only going to slow you down so fast. Whatever you do, don't run into the dock."

"Wait, what are you going to be doing?"

"Trying to save Caine."

Jerek turned and ran to the other side of the boat, throwing himself off in what I was sure was a suicidal move, but as his feet left the boat, dark planes of energy sprouted from his back and formed bat-like wings.

The shock of seeing him fly—even after all the other crazy things I'd seen happen so far that day—was so overpowering that I almost didn't get the boat turned in time to avoid slamming full speed into the floating dock.

Despite my almost complete focus on Jerek, I managed to cut the throttle back at the same time I steered hard to the right. The pain was excruciating, but that didn't stop me from seeing Jerek fly more than fifty feet without touching the water. As impressive as that was, it was apparent to me that he was struggling to stay airborne. When you got right down to it, his initial jump plus that first downward sweep of his wings was what got him all of the height he managed to obtain. After that, it seemed as though all his wings did was slow his fall.

Jerek was only three or four feet off of the ground when he made it to Caine and the two hunters, but he carried a surprising amount of speed with him, and he led with his feet when he slammed into the closest of the two hunters with enough force that I was pretty sure he'd just snapped the creature's back. That had the benefit of bleeding off most of Jerek's momentum, but he still hit the ground hard enough that I half worried he'd broken something in the process.

Jerek tumbled more than twenty feet before coming to a stop, but he bounced right back up, which was a good thing given that the remaining creature had abandoned its attempt to kill Caine so that it could make it to Jerek before he'd recovered from his crash landing. I brought the boat around as I passed the dock, making sure that I was still able to see the fight, and my heart leapt up into my throat as Jerek engaged the creature all by himself.

There was a different feel to this fight. It seemed like Jerek was waging a fighting retreat in an attempt to let Caine make it over to him so that the two of them could double-team the hunter. Rather than aggressively attacking the creature, Jerek was dodging every blow he could, and for the ones he couldn't dodge he was blocking the strikes with his hands and arms. Apparently whatever mystical armor had been protecting him earlier was still functioning on those parts of his body.

The fact that Jerek had managed to make it nearly fifteen seconds without being marked up by the hunter was a testimony to his raw speed and skill, but I could see that he was starting to tire. Just before Caine made it over to him, he missed a block and the creature opened up a matching set of cuts to Jerek's leg. I was pretty sure that the same blow would've cut my leg completely free of my body, so the fact that Jerek didn't lose his limb entirely was a testament to the strength of his inhuman constitution. Despite that, the slices in his leg looked deep—maybe even life-threatening.

Jerek went down on one knee as his right leg refused to support his weight, and the creature surged forward, sensing an opportunity to end the fight before Caine could close with it. I thought Jerek was a goner, but at the last second he conjured the same bat-like wings I'd seen a few moments earlier and used them to block the creature's attack. My breath caught in my chest as the wings shredded under the force of the creature's blow, and then Caine was there with his arms around the hunter's neck. He snapped the creature's vertebrae with a single explosive movement and then dropped down to the ground next to Jerek, obviously spent.

With the death of the second creature, the high-school kids who'd been passively watching the fight started to come out of the daze the creature had put them under, but Jerek rolled over and fixed the closest guy with a stare.

"Go get one of your friends and bring them over here. You don't remember anything you just saw, just that you're disappointed that the party turned out to be such a bust."

Caine groaned, but worked himself up into a sitting position, oblivious to the dust and blood staining his torso. By the time Caine was standing once again, Jerek's first puppet was back with another guy who looked like he was on the football team.

By that point I was too focused on trying to maneuver Jerek's boat up to the dock to catch most of what was said, but when I looked up again two of my classmates were standing there to help make sure I didn't cave in the side of the boat as I brought it up to the dock. Another pair of guys had jumped into the boat we'd originally taken from the mainland to the island, and there was another group of people helping Jerek to his feet.

"We're supposed to help you onto the dock and then take the boat to go get the people still at Jerek's house. Will you let us help you?"

The guy who was asking me the question said it with such lifelessness that I would've known something was up even if I hadn't seen Jerek and Caine using their compulsion on people earlier in the night. The closest of the pair offered me his hand as his companion climbed into the boat, but I shook my head and moved to the far end so that I could climb out without being touched by someone who no longer seemed to have a will of his own.

I hurried across the dock, headed towards Jerek and Caine. Maybe the smartest thing to do would've been to run the other direction given that the two of them seemed to be in the middle of every freaky thing that had happened since I'd arrived in Clay, but I didn't have a way home. More importantly, there still a chance there were more of those pale monsters in the area.

I would have been lying though if I'd said that was the only reason I didn't run in the opposite direction from Caine and Jerek. More than just being scared for my life, I also very much wanted to get to the bottom of what I'd just seen. I've never been one to believe in werewolves or vampires, but I wasn't about to argue with my own eyes, not when combined with all of the other inexplicable happenings over the last few days. I wanted answers.

Caine looked like he'd lost even more blood than I'd realized. He was trying to disconnect the boat trailer from Jerek's SUV, and was obviously struggling too much for such a simple task. I went over intending to help, but Jerek got there first. He was being supported on either side by beefy football players who looked like they were still struggling to support his weight despite their considerable muscles, but he was mobile, and obviously in a hurry.

"Get out of the way, Caine. We don't have time to screw around. That's three of them we've run into today who had no discernible scent. For all we know, there are twenty more headed this way right now."

I opened my mouth to ask what Jerek was going to do given just how bad off he was, but while I was still looking for the right words Caine took several steps to the side. A moment later Jerek lashed out with a kick to the tongue of the boat trailer. The shriek as the metal hitch broke made my skin crawl. More importantly though, it begged the question of just what exactly the hunters were made out of that they'd been able to withstand so much punishment from Jerek and Caine before finally succumbing to their wounds.

Jerek was swaying on his feet now, obviously having exerted himself too far, but he turned around and sighed in relief when he saw me standing a little ways behind him. "Good, Dani, you're okay. Go get Caine's keys from him and take his car somewhere safe."

"Somewhere safe? I don't have the foggiest idea what just happened, how am I supposed to know if some place is safe?"

"Get to the middle of the country—someplace without any big bodies of water. Iowa, Ohio or Nebraska all come to mind. If you go right now, you should be able to make it out of their reach before you get too tired to drive. Caine can give you a prepaid credit card that will see you through at least the next day or two. After that we'll make sure we send you additional funds."

Jerek had such a commanding presence—even when obviously injured and unable to stand on his own—that I made it all of the way over to Caine and accepted his keys and wallet before I realized that obeying his orders would end up with me alone, lost in an unfamiliar state, without any idea what was going on back in Wisconsin.

"No, I'm not going anywhere."

Caine reached towards me as though wanting to say something, but Jerek beat him to it. "It's not safe here, Dani. If you stay here you're going to die, and I don't want that on my conscience."

"What about all of them?" I pointed at the teenagers who were slowly moving towards their cars as though still in a daze. "What about my dad?"

"They are probably safe—your dad too. The hunters feed off of human emotions. They're going to look at all of these people as a food source, but they're mostly going to want to keep them alive. That's not the case for us, though, and I'm betting it's not the case for you either. You're almost as impervious to what the hunters do to the human mind as you are to our compulsion. If they can't immobilize you, then they can't feed on you, and there's no reason for them to keep you alive."

Jerek motioned for his human crutches to help him climb into the SUV. I'd been expecting him to continue giving me reasons why I had to leave, but apparently as far as Jerek was concerned the matter was settled. I turned to Caine and he nodded.

"He's telling the truth, Dani. I don't know what you are, but you're not a regular person. I'm hoping that Jerek is blowing all of this out of proportion, but if he's right and there are more hunters out there, the three of us won't last two minutes in our current state. Our only hope—your only hope—is to get on the road and not stop until we're far enough away from here that there's no way they could've followed us."

"Fine, I can't stay here, but I'm not running away without my dad. I'll call him on my way home—odds are that he'll be home within minutes of me getting there and we can be on the road before the hour is out."

"Grab her and get her into the SUV."

I thought for a second that Jerek was talking to Caine, but one look confirmed that Caine was just as shocked as I was. A split second later several sets of hands latched onto my arms and I realized that Jerek was capable of a lot more in the way of compulsion than I'd realized. Not only did he still have control of the two football players supporting him, he'd also reached out and compelled two more guys to restrain me.

I kicked and screamed, but there were two of them and they each outweighed me by more than sixty pounds. It was like a one-week-old kitten trying to break away from a pair of Saint Bernards. Everything happened so quickly that

I'd been frogmarched halfway to Jerek's vehicle before Caine managed to react.

"What are you doing, Jerek? This is crazy!"

"I'm doing what has to be done. We can't compel her, and we can't trust her to do as she's told. The last thing I want is for her and my mother to meet, but the only way to ensure that she's safe is for her to come with us. Put her in the driver's seat."

The guys holding my arms reacted with the emotionless movements of robots, opening the SUV door and cramming me into the vehicle despite everything I could do to fight them. Jerek—still assisted by the two football players he'd been using as human crutches—slid into the seat behind me as Caine stumbled around to the passenger side of the SUV.

Jerek started to motion for the football players to go help Caine, who was obviously on his last legs, but Caine waved them off, pulling himself into the car with bloody hands and then slouching in his seat while trying to hold the worst of the wounds in his gut closed with his arm.

"Jerek, you need to let Dani go. I know that there are risks, but you can't kidnap her."

The words came out slurred and weak, and despite all of the craziness I'd witnessed since the first of the creatures had attacked Jerek and I back on the island, it was only Caine's pale skin and labored breathing that finally made me realize this wasn't some kind of movie. There were no doctors waiting in the wings, and I had no idea how far away the closest hospital was. It was entirely possible that Caine was going to die before my eyes.

Jerek was yelling at me to get the SUV moving, but I could barely make out his words over the thundering of my own pulse in my ears. I stabbed the engine start button with a finger and dropped the vehicle into gear as I scanned for the exit from the parking lot.

"Promise me that you'll let her go, Jerek. If our friendship means anything to you, anything at all, you won't do this to her. She'll never forgive us."

"Your friendship means more to me than you know, Caine, but I have responsibilities that even you don't know about. I will keep our people's secret and keep her safe regardless of the cost to you or me personally. Change now while you still have a chance."

Caine coughed and there was blood on his lips that hadn't been there just seconds before. Taking my eyes off of the road while racing through a parking lot was asking to get in a wreck, but I couldn't seem to tear my eyes away from Caine.

He gave me a sad smile and for once there was no hint of teasing or laughter in his eyes. "I'm sorry, Dani. I'm afraid I'm out of time."

Caine closed his eyes and stopped breathing.

Chapter 5

My scream was deafening, and I still wasn't looking at the road, but I didn't care. I'd only known Caine for a couple of days, but that didn't make his death any less terrifying. I gasped, drawing in more air to continue screaming, and then Jerek was there, reaching around each side of the seat, one hand on the steering wheel, the other grabbing my arm and stretching it toward Caine's body.

"He's not dead. Feel his shoulder."

Even as he spoke, Jerek wrenched the wheel to the side, slewing the heavy vehicle around so that we were no longer headed directly toward a light post. My hands had been locked in a death grip on the steering wheel, but Jerek tore them free like it was nothing.

Under other circumstances, I would have been worried he was going to rip the light material of my jacket. He certainly left bruises on my arms, and there was a flare of pain from my sprained wrist, but all of that paled in comparison from what my fingertips were reporting.

Caine still wasn't breathing, but he didn't feel like a dead body, he felt like a granite sculpture. I'd noticed that he was all solid muscle before this, but that was nothing like what I was feeling at that moment. It was like he'd been transformed into living rock between one heartbeat and the next, a transformation that was just as shocking as thinking he was dead had been.

I slammed my foot on the brake pedal, bringing the SUV to a screeching halt, and then turned around in my seat. "What's going on?"

Jerek looked nearly as pale as Caine had been, and a tiny part of me registered that there was now blood all over my jacket.

"I'll explain everything once we're on the freeway, but we really need to get moving again, Dani. Every minute we stay here puts the people in this area in that much more danger. The hunters prefer to keep humans alive if at all possible, but under the right circumstances they are perfectly capable of using your kind to try to kill my kind. As weakened as I am, I won't be able to counter that kind of mass compulsion. Please start driving again."

"Caine is going to be okay?"

"I can't guarantee anything, but the odds are heavily in his favor."

I met Jerek's eyes and there was something there that made me believe him. He was telling the truth about Caine, and I was even pretty sure that he was telling the truth about the hunters. That didn't excuse him essentially kidnapping me, but he was getting paler by the minute. I didn't need to fight him or argue him into letting me go, I just needed to wait for him to pass out—or whatever it was that he and Caine did when they approached death—and then I would be free to do whatever I wanted.

It was odd in a way. I really did believe Jerek when he said that I was putting myself in danger by staying in Wisconsin, but that didn't matter as much as the fact that I wasn't going to leave my dad in danger while I ran away somewhere safe.

"Okay, I'll start driving again, but I want an explanation."

I reached for the steering wheel again and Jerek let go and pulled his hands back so quickly it was almost like he thought I was carrying the plague.

"I'm sure you do, but I'm afraid any kind of explanation is going to have to wait until later."

Jerek was doing his best to act nonchalant, but something in his voice told me he was up to something. Unfortunately, I realized that too late, and he pulled my phone out of the pocket in my jacket before I could stop him.

"Give me my phone back!"

I reached behind me, blindly trying to grab his hand—for all the good it would do me—but Jerek threw himself back into the aisle between the seats in something that was halfway between a lunge and a drunken fall. He was fading fast, and I realized that there was more of a chance than I'd initially realized that I might be able to overpower him.

I slammed on the brakes again, fully intending on climbing back there and taking my phone back, but Jerek was already dialing a number.

"Mr. Destone, I need you to stop what you're doing and listen to me very carefully."

The all-too-familiar pressure was back hammering against the inside of my skull, but this time I could tell that I wasn't the target of Jerek's compulsion—my dad was.

"What are you doing, Jerek?"

"You're far too crafty for your own good, Dani, and not nearly as sneaky as you think you are. I could see it in your eyes when you decided you were just going to wait until I changed and then ditch Caine and me. If you really care about your father, you need to keep driving."

By that point the SUV had stopped and I was halfway out of my seat, but with every word out of Jerek's mouth I became more and more convinced that my efforts were futile.

"Mr. Destone, please get into your car and drive south. You can stop and rest when you are tired, but other than stopping to rest or refuel, you must drive straight through until you reach Ohio. Once there, pick a random town in the state and stay there for the next week. You will not worry about Dani, and you will not call the police or do anything else to create a scene."

Nothing Jerek had said so far was overtly hostile, but I'd already dropped back down into my seat. I could already see where things were headed, and any doubt I might have had was erased as Jerek met my eyes again.

"It's vitally important that you listen to me, Mr. Destone, ignore everything else so that you can focus on my words. Dani needs to stay with me. If she calls without me, or if she calls from anywhere other than Utah, I want you to step out into traffic and ensure that you are killed. If Dani and I don't call together within the next week, then drive your car into the nearest river and stay inside it until you pass out."

Jerek looked at me with cold, emotionless eyes as he switched my phone to speaker. "Do you understand your instructions, Mr. Destone?"

"Yes, I understand and I will comply."

Jerek hung up on my dad without ever looking away from me. "I'm going to lose consciousness in the next few seconds, but your father's life—and the lives of tens of thousands of other people—depends on you getting Caine and me to Utah in time to stop the hunters from taking over the entire area."

Chapter 6

It shouldn't have surprised me that Jerek closed his eyes and turned to stone before I could get a response out. The SUV looked like a murder scene and if anything Jerek had taken more damage than Caine, but that didn't make my choice any easier.

I slid my phone out of Jerek's fingers and debated calling my dad, but I'd felt Jerek's compulsion while he'd been on the phone. There had been moments when it had been stronger than other times, but I had zero doubt but that my dad was going to die if I called him. Just like he was going to die if we didn't make it to Utah quickly enough.

Much as I didn't like it, my hands were tied. I put the SUV back into gear and called up Utah on the GPS. I hit the interstate even more quickly than I'd been expecting, and despite a bladder that felt like it was going to explode, I stayed on the road until the computer said that we were down to less than twenty miles of fuel left.

It wasn't late enough in the year to be freezing yet, but by the time two in the morning hit it was cold enough that I was missing being able to wear my jacket—the one that Jerek had gotten all bloody. I pumped gas in a nearly deserted truck stop with my teeth chattering in nothing more than my board shorts and a T-shirt, and I cursed Jerek the entire time.

By the time Jerek finally woke up I'd been driving for nearly eight hours and I was so far beyond pissed that it was all I could do to keep from screaming at him.

"Where are we?"

Jerek asked the question as he moved forward to the seat directly behind Caine.

"We're less than an hour outside of Omaha, Nebraska."

"Caine hasn't woken up yet?"

I looked over in time to see Jerek place two fingers on the side of Caine's neck. It was an odd gesture considering that Caine still seemed to be carved out of solid granite, but that was nothing compared to all of the other crazy things I'd seen since we'd been attacked on Madeline Island.

"No. I assumed the fact that he is still as hard as a rock was a good sign. Should I have been worried?"

My concern for Caine was strong enough to bleed past even my anger at Jerek, but not by much. Caine hadn't been the one to kidnap me, but he'd lured me into a world I didn't understand, one that had ended up being dangerous for more than just me. Whether he'd meant to put my dad and me in danger or not, we were going to have a long talk once he woke up.

"No, as long as he's still in a healing trance there isn't much call to worry. If the worst had come to pass and his body wasn't able to heal itself, there wouldn't have been much you could have done anyway."

"You're awful casual about the idea of Caine dying. Does he know how little he matters to you?"

The sheer venom in my voice surprised even me—not that I was feeling it, but that I'd actually come right out for once and said what I was thinking. I didn't get much of a chance to feel proud about my assertiveness though because Jerek turned on me instantly.

"Caine means more to me than you can possibly understand. What you heard in my voice just now wasn't indifference, it was resignation. I'm sorry that you got caught up in the war between my people and the hunters, but unlike you, I didn't just stumble into this conflict, I was born into it. I've seen dozens of people I cared about go off to Jerusalem or South America and never come back.

"The last thing I want is to watch Caine die. In fact, I was so determined to save him that I nearly got myself killed jumping out of that boat, but that doesn't change reality. Like it or not, there isn't anything else I can do to save him but make sure that we get to Salt Lake as quickly as possible."

Jerek's response was full of so much anger that my rage flickered, but it roared back even stronger before he'd finished talking.

"Was that supposed to be an apology? I couldn't tell. I heard the word 'sorry' in there, but you failed to acknowledge having done anything wrong. Do you even remember compelling my father to kill himself? If you're really going to start apologizing for things, you should start with that."

"Pull the car over, Dani."

"I knew you weren't actually sorry about anything. Do you know that I've been sitting here behind this wheel for the last eight hours trying to come up with a reason that justified you acting like such a complete prick?"

"Dani, I'm—"

"Don't you dare interrupt me! Believe it or not, that's exactly what I've been doing—not because I care one way or the other about you, but for Caine's sake. He seems like an honest-to-goodness decent guy and based on the fact that he was against kidnapping me, I can only imagine how disappointed he's going to be when he wakes up and finds out that you've been using my own father against me like some kind of Third World drug lord."

"If you'll just hear—"

All of the anger had leached out of Jerek's voice, but I was too pissed to register his conciliatory tone.

"Fine, you can drive."

Still too angry to think, I spun the steering wheel to the right and stomped on the brakes so hard that Jerek was thrown forward with enough force that anyone else probably would have gone through the windshield.

Fortunately—for Jerek at least—he wasn't just some guy. He managed to latch onto Caine's chair with his right hand before completely losing his balance. Jerek clamped down on the chair hard enough to make the metal frame groan in distress, and he still put a hole in the dash, but he somehow kept himself from being ejected from the car, which would have impressed me if not for the fact that his left hand brushed my bare arm as it flew by.

It was like being hit in the face by a basketball—something that had happened in my last school while one of the jocks had been trying to show off in front of his friends. The physical impact of Jerek's knuckles grazing my arm was bad enough to leave bruises on my arm, but that was nothing compared to the shock that raced up my arm and then exploded inside my skull like twenty tons of dynamite.

If we hadn't already been slowing down, I probably would have wrecked the SUV, which should have terrified me, but the jolt inside my head seemed to have left me numb. It was like all of the emotions that had been raging inside of me evaporated between one instant and the next.

Nothing else had changed. All of the circumstances still justified me being angry. He'd kidnapped me, threatened to make my dad kill himself, and shown a complete lack of concern over my wellbeing. I knew I should be mad, but I just couldn't summon any kind of emotion, which was all the more interesting in comparison to Jerek's reaction, a reaction that I was able to observe with the cool detachment of a scientist.

Jerek gasped like he'd just been punched in the gut at the same time that the chair he was holding groaned again as though only heartbeats from being ripped free from its moorings. He was shaking as he recoiled from me with the kind of speed usually reserved for people who accidentally touched stove burners.

"What just happened?"

My emotions were still MIA so there wasn't any real curiosity behind the question, but my intellect was screaming non-stop that some-thing so unusual—even coming on the tail end of more than twenty-four hours of one crazy thing after another—demanded explanation.

"I don't know—I can't explain it."

He was still shaking as he spoke, and I got the sense it was all he could do not to act on the hurricane of emotions apparently raging inside of him, but even past that it was obvious that he was hedging his bets. There was something in his eyes that should have made me profoundly uncomfortable, but in my present state I was able to look past that and see the measuring, contemplative tilt to his head.

"You just lied to me. Why can't I feel the anger something like that deserves?"

"I didn't lie. I've never heard of something like that happening. I had a suspicion that it would be a bad idea for you and me to spend much time around each other, but I didn't anticipate that things would degenerate quite so quickly. Do you remember what we were fighting about?"

I nodded. "You kidnapped me and then compelled my dad to kill himself if I didn't get you and Caine to Utah. If I could still feel my emotions, I would probably be trying to claw your face off, but you've rather neatly solved that problem. I love—or at least I used to love—my dad more than I hate you."

"You would be justified to hate me. I would tell you that I didn't feel like I had any other choice, that I knew I only had minutes before I was going to have to lapse into a healing trance if I were going to have any chance of surviving. I would tell you that the survival of tens—or possibly even hundreds—of thousands of people depends on Caine and I making it to Utah as quickly as possible, but we both know that doesn't justify compelling someone you love to hurt themselves if you failed to follow my orders.

"The only thing I can say is that I'm sorry. I never actually compelled your father to do all of the things you think I did, but that doesn't change the fact that I regret what I had to do to you."

The emotionless computer that was now my mind weighed all of the information and arrived at a verdict I never would have entertained if my feelings hadn't been so muted.

Jerek was telling the truth.

"How did you do it?"

"Partway through the conversation I told him to 'ignore everything else' as I surged the compulsion up to the strongest level I can manage, and then I dropped the compulsion down when I told him to hurt himself if anything happened to us. The stronger compulsion made him ignore almost the entire last half of our conversation, which means he was never in any real danger—at least not from me."

"You got him to safety at the same time that you ensured my compliance. Very slick. I'm not sure I'll be able to feel the same way if my emotions ever come back, but at least right now I can appreciate the elegance of your solution."

Jerek nodded, and only my state of detachment allowed me to tell that things weren't back to normal for him yet. He was doing a good job pretending otherwise, but there was still some kind of fire raging inside of him, one that had come within inches of consuming him before he managed to get it at least partially under control.

Acting on instinct, I reached out and grabbed Jerek's arm, moving with a suddenness that exceeded anything I was normally capable of, which was the only reason I managed to take him by surprise. Jerek recoiled away from me again, falling into the very back row of seats, but by then I'd already assimilated the results of my experiment.

"It doesn't happen every time."

Jerek rubbed his arm where I'd touched him and nodded. "The shock at least seems to be irregular. That was a risky thing to try though. What if touching again had resulted in your emotions being even more damaged?"

I shrugged. Now that my feelings were gone, the prospect of going through life like this wasn't as terrifying as it would have been under other circumstances. Living like this would doubtlessly result in a whole new level of difficulty when it came to connecting with other people, but truth be told I'd already been living a pretty solitary existence. The biggest difference now was that I just wouldn't feel any loneliness.

"It seemed worth it at the time. So where do we go from here?"

"Unless you're opposed to the idea, I think we should trade out. The healing trance isn't as restful as real sleep, but I'm good to drive for a few hours while you sleep. I've still got some internal damage that will need to be dealt with at some point, but if you don't get some sleep you're likely to wreck and then we'll all end up dead anyway."

I didn't need to do any kind of internal survey to know that he was right about just how exhausted I was. I'd considered pulling off at a gas station and trying to get some sleep several times in the previous hour, so his plan made a lot of sense—especially when combined with the fact that I didn't feel like I needed to prove anything to him or Caine.

It felt like maybe the faintest tendril of pride was trying to re-manifest somewhere deep down in my gut, but if so it was still a long ways away from being a strong enough emotion to influence my behavior. Still, it was a good sign. Emotionless me wasn't sure that emotions were everything they were cracked up to be, but I didn't want one more thing differentiating me from everyone else.

"Okay, I'll trade you seats and try to go to sleep, but only if you promise to wake me up if you get tired or your injuries start affecting you."

"Of course. More than just our survival hinges on Caine and I getting safely to Utah."

Part of me wanted to know what he meant by that—either because my curiosity was trying to make a comeback, or simply because even this cold, calculating version of me knew that I needed more information if I was going to survive in this new, dangerous world I'd just been thrust into. In the end, I decided against asking more questions simply because of the sheer weight of the exhaustion pulling at me, but it was a close thing.

Once Jerek was safely repositioned in the driver's seat and I was sprawled out across the back seat, he dropped the SUV back into gear and pulled back onto the interstate. Less than half an hour previously I would have said that I would never be calm enough around Jerek—after what I'd thought he'd done to my father—to fall asleep while he was conscious and in the same car with me, but that was no longer an issue.

I was nearly asleep when one final question flittered across my mind.

"How long before Caine wakes up?"

"I don't know—probably a while still, but hopefully he'll wake up before I need someone to spell me."

"I guess it makes sense that it would take Caine longer to finish healing—he was hurt worse, so he had to shift into a healing trance before you. It only follows that it would take him longer to heal. The funny thing is that I initially thought you were hurt worse than he was."

"I was."

There was an odd note in Jerek's voice, but I was far too tired to identify it. It was all I could do to push out one more question and try to hold on to consciousness for long enough to hear his response. "How come you were able to wake up first then?"

"We all have our crosses to carry, Dani."

Chapter 7

I slept for much longer than I would have expected given just how hard I'd always found it to sleep while in a car. Jerek's SUV had a roomier back seat than I was used to, but I suspected that it was more the result of just how tired I'd been when I'd finally nodded off. Apparently that kind of extreme terror took even more out of a person than I'd realized.

I stretched my neck from side to side—trying to work out a kink—as I looked out the window. The sun was well above the horizon. No wonder I was hungry.

Once I turned away from the window, I saw that Caine was now driving, and Jerek had taken up a position in one of the two middle seats. Based on the fact that he didn't seem to be breathing, it was a pretty good bet that he was deep in another healing trance.

Caine looked up at the rear-view mirror and smiled when he saw me sitting up. "Good morning, sleepy head. How are you feeling?"

"Still tired, sore, and hungry—maybe not in that order though. Are you completely healed then?"

"Yep, as good as new. You want to join me up here? Jerek moved back there so that you could have the passenger seat—he thought it might make talking easier."

"Also it would mean that we weren't yelling at each other to communicate, thus making it more likely that he would be able to continue sleeping, or trancing, or whatever it is you guys do. By the way, what *are* you?"

Caine shot me a rare frown. "Jerek wasn't thinking about himself. In his current state you could set off a firecracker next to his ear and he would never hear a thing. He really was trying to make it easier for you and me to talk to each other."

I bit back a hot retort—which told me that my feelings were starting to return to their normal state—and reminded myself that Caine hadn't been the one to threaten my father. Caine and I still might be headed into choppy water, but there was no reason to go borrowing trouble before he'd even had a chance to express an opinion one way or the other.

I took a deep breath and then opened my mouth intending on asking once again what I'd gotten myself into when I became friends with Caine, but before I could get the words out a new torrent of emotions slammed into me.

"Caine, how do I know that Jerek was telling the truth? What if he lied about not compelling my dad?"

I went from composed to crying in just a couple heartbeats and could feel a complete breakdown hovering in the wings. It was hard to say whether the strength of my reaction to the thought of my dad still being in danger was somehow tied to my emotions being suppressed for a period of time, or if the situation had just triggered something even stronger than the worry and anger that I'd felt the night before prior to Jerek brushing against my arm. All I knew was that I wasn't going to be able to hold things together for much longer.

I'd stumbled towards the front of the SUV as I'd started crying, and Caine reached back tenderly to guide me into the battered chair next to him.

"Jerek is a lot of things, but there is absolutely no way that he really compelled your dad to kill himself and then lied about it after the fact. He told me all about what happened while I was out and I absolutely believe that your dad is just fine.

"What's going on, Dani? It sounded to me like you believed Jerek earlier when he told you it had all just been a ruse to make sure you didn't go running off without us..."

"I did, but that was back when my emotions were MIA. Now that they are making a comeback, it's harder to be so analytical about everything. I think the thing that probably sent me over the edge just now is that there isn't any way for me to really know that Dad's okay. If I call by myself and Jerek was lying about not compelling my dad to kill himself, then I'll never see him again."

"But if you call with Jerek on the phone then all bets are off because Jerek can compel him to do whatever he wants."

I nodded, and then scowled at Caine's relieved shrug. "Are you condoning what Jerek did, because if so—"

"Hold on—as I was about to say, you don't need to worry about anything. I will call your dad, compel him not to hurt himself—just in case I'm wrong about Jerek, even though I know I'm not—and then hand the phone over to you. You'll know that I'm not pulling any kind of funny business because I'll only get a chance to say that one thing, and then you'll be able to talk to your dad to your heart's content."

"Will that really work? Can you counteract Jerek's earlier orders?"

"Please, sister. Jerek is pretty hot stuff, but the number of people who can put down a compulsion that I can't override are few enough that

I can count them on two hands. I can break any compulsion Jerek might have put on your dad and not even break a sweat."

It wasn't foolproof, or rather it was only foolproof if I trusted Caine completely. I was still crying, which I would have expected to throw off my usual tells enough that Caine wouldn't be able to read me as easily as he normally could, but either more of my suspicions made it to my face than I realized, or I just took too long to express the combination of relief and gratitude he was expecting.

"If you're worried that I'm going to say one thing on the phone while compelling him to do something else, you don't need to sweat that possibility. When we're face to face with someone it's possible to compel them without words—or even to say one thing while compelling them to do something else entirely—but once we're no longer in close proximity to them we have to have words to focus their thoughts on what we want them to do."

Caine still hadn't told me what he and Jerek were—I was long past convinced they couldn't be human—but that was an interesting piece of information nonetheless. Unfortunately, it didn't actually change the situation I was facing. It all boiled down to whether I could trust Caine.

If I trusted him, then it didn't matter how compulsion worked over long distances because he would do exactly as promised. If, however, I didn't trust Caine, then all of the assurances in the world wouldn't make the slightest bit of difference.

I sat there in silence for so long that eventually Caine took his eyes off the road again to give me a questioning look. Part of me wanted to lump Caine in with Jerek, but the fact of the matter was that Caine had never been anything but good to me, and I'd never caught him in even the smallest lie. Right or wrong, I trusted Caine—trusted him with my life or my father's life either one.

"Okay, let's do it."

I dialed my dad's number and then held the phone up to Caine's ear so that he wouldn't have to look away from the road.

"Don't hurt yourself, Mr. Destone."

The sense of pressure I'd learned to associate with compulsion was back and this time it was so thick it almost felt suffocating. I wasn't entirely sure that my natural resistance to having my mind manipulated would have been enough to protect me this time around if Caine had been targeting me, but it was obvious that Caine's efforts were focused elsewhere.

I didn't remember Caine ever directing that kind of power at me before, which meant one of two things. Either my internal sensors were still partially on the fritz from whatever had happened when Jerek and I had touched, or Caine had really pulled out the stops to make sure that my dad would be safe.

I suspected it was more the latter, which was beyond touching—especially given just how much it seemed to take out of Caine. He was slumped in his chair looking like someone who'd just gone thirty-six hours straight without any sleep, but true to his word, he motioned for me to take the phone back without saying anything else that could be used to further compel my dad.

I'd stopped crying shortly after deciding that I still trusted Caine despite everything else that had happened, but I was shaking again as I brought the phone back to my ear.

"Are you there, Daddy?"

"Dani, is that really you? Where are you, and what is going on?"

The distress in his voice made my throat tighten up, and before I could respond he launched into another round of questions, most of which I didn't really have answers for.

"Who did I talk to last night, and why do I find myself obeying his instructions over my better judgment? Most of all, why am I not worried about you? I haven't seen you in more than a day, and I have no idea where you are or who you're with. That's the kind of thing that should have me beside myself with concern, but I can't seem to muster up any kind of emotional response regarding you and whether you're safe. That's not natural!"

"Please calm down, Dad."

"Calm down? Don't tell me to calm down! Something is majorly wrong and I don't know what to do about it."

Things were spiraling out of control much more quickly than I would have believed possible. "Dad, I'm trying to tell you what's going on—at least as much as I know—but you're not giving me a chance to get a word in edgewise. I need you to answer one question for me, and then I'll tell you everything."

"Fine. I'll answer your question and then you can finally start answering mine. Start with telling me where you are."

"Okay. I know that the first guy you talked to—the one from last night—told you to go to Ohio, and he told you not to worry about me. Did he tell you anything else?"

"He told me to go to a random town and await further instruction. Why, were you not there with him?"

"That's it? He didn't tell you to hurt yourself if I called back without him?"

"Don't be absurd, Dani, where is this coming from?"

"Please, Dad, just answer the question. Do you remember him saying anything about what you were supposed to do if he wasn't on the phone with me when I called you, anything at all?"

"No, nothing like that happened. He told me to go to Ohio and then after a long pause he asked me if I understood my orders."

I wasn't trembling on the outside anymore, but the fluttery feeling of relief coursing through me was so strong that I was astonished it hadn't started me shaking again. Jerek had deceived me, threatening my dad in order to make sure that I would stay with him and Caine, but he hadn't actually ever put my dad in any danger. He hadn't been lying to me when he'd confessed just before I'd gone to sleep.

In the grand scheme of things maybe what he'd done still merited my eternal hatred, but I wasn't positive of that fact anymore. I'd seen the hunters with my own eyes, and everything from their wicked-looking claws to the cunning intelligence I'd sensed while Jerek fought the one back by the pool had pointed toward them being predators who were perfectly happy to feed on people.

I still didn't particularly approve of Jerek's methods. I would have much preferred he simply take the time to tell me what was going on. I've always been a pretty reasonable girl, so once I really understood the stakes I probably would have cooperated with him, but then again he'd been operating under a pretty severe time constraint.

If I was correctly reading the situation and what was on the line, then lots of people had done things that were much worse for ends that weren't nearly as compelling and still been vindicated by historians. That was a big 'if' though. I simply didn't know enough about what was really going on to say for sure if I would have done the same thing in Jerek's place.

"You promised to start answering my questions, Dani. Where are you?"

"I'm three quarters of the way to Utah, and—"

"Turn around and come back home immediately! I'll figure out how to overcome whatever it is that's keeping me from going back to Wisconsin and then once we're both safe again we can talk about how long you're going to be grounded for after pulling such a harebrained stunt."

"I'm sorry, but I can't do that, Dad."

"Why not? Are those guys you're with holding you against your will?"

I opened my mouth to answer and then realized that I didn't know how to respond. I covered the receiver as I looked over at Caine. He shook his head.

"You can go whenever you need to."

"Really? Is Jerek going to be okay with that?"

Caine shrugged. "Jerek is acting a little crazy right now, but now that we're both out of danger I think he'll be okay with it."

"I'm not so sure about that."

"Then I'll just drop you off right now. Jerek is healing, and by the time he wakes up you'll be a couple hundred miles behind us and have had at least a couple of hours to lengthen your lead.

I'll give you enough money to buy a car and go wherever you want to go.

"I trust you not to say anything about what you saw back at the house, and given the circumstances, it's not like he's going to waste time turning around and trying to hunt you down. No offense intended, but there are way bigger issues at stake right now."

There it was, everything laid out nice and neat, just like I'd spent so much time wishing it could be on the long drive from Wisconsin to Nebraska. I wasn't as sure as Caine that Jerek would just let me go without looking for me—I couldn't have said why though—but Caine was right about one thing. If I wanted to go find my dad, there wasn't anything stopping me now.

My dad had shown impressive restraint given what had to be going through his head right now, but even just a couple of seconds of silence had strained his nerves to the breaking point.

"Dani, are you still there?"

"Yeah, Dad, I'm still here."

"Well, are you being held against your will?"

His tone said that he was pretty sure I wasn't, but I still had to answer him.

"No, I'm free to go whenever I want."

"Then I want you to turn that car around and get yourself back here pronto, young lady."

"I'm sorry, Dad, I can't do that."

Even just a few seconds before, I wouldn't have been able to say why I was going to stick it out with Caine and Jerek, but now it was perfectly clear what I had to do. More than just worry and anger had reawakened inside of me while I'd been asleep, and my curiosity had grown to the point of being nearly overpowering.

"I'll call the police and report that you're missing. Those kids you're with will go to jail for kidnapping and then you'll spend the next year—"

I handed the phone to Caine. "Please calm him down."

"Is that all you want?"

"I'm not sure. I want to be able to talk to him and explain my decision, but I don't want him so messed up that he's not really himself anymore."

"Okay, one defanged parent coming right up." Caine visibly steeled himself, tapping hidden reserves of strength to replenish the energy he'd expended making sure that my dad wouldn't hurt himself. "Mr. Destone, you're not allowed to hang up on me or your daughter, and you have to listen to everything I say. You're not going to call the police, or tell anyone that anything unusual is happening with Dani. You're not allowed to yell at her or talk over her. In short, you're going to have to hear her out. You can worry about her if you want though."

Caine gave me a tired smile as he handed the phone back to me. "There you go. He's as normal as he's going to get short of my telling him he can go back to Wisconsin. I can do that too, but I thought I should check with you first before I did that."

I accepted my phone with a nod of thanks. "I can't explain everything that's going on right now, Dad, but I'm in the middle of something that I want to see through to the end."

"How is any of this possible, Dani? These guys you're with keep telling me stuff and it's like I don't have any say in the matter. How are they doing this?"

"I'm not sure. They call it compulsion, and frankly it's the least bizarre thing I've seen in the last twenty-four hours."

"By bizarre you mean dangerous, don't you?"

"Yeah, I guess I do."

My dad was silent for several seconds as he considered his response. "I'm not going to be able to convince you to come back home, am I?"

"I don't think so, Dad. I understand why you're worried—I really do—but this is just something that I need to see through to the end. I promise that I'll be as careful as I can be though."

"It goes without saying that I don't like it, Dani, but given the circumstances, my hands are pretty much tied. I can't call the cops or even tell anyone there is something crazy happening to the two of us, so trying to reason with you was my only hope. I should have realized from the start that wasn't going to work.

"Your mom used to sound exactly like this when she decided that she wasn't going to be

swayed off of her chosen path. I've been sus-
pecting for a couple of years that you inherited
her stubbornness, but it's never been quite so
obvious until now just how much you take after
her in that way."

I felt tears returning to my eyes. "I miss her
too, Dad."

"I know. You're all I have left of her though,
so please be careful."

"I will. Do you want to know anything else
about what's going on?"

He paused for several seconds before clearing
his throat. "Not unless you have something you
need my advice about. Regardless of my feelings
about what's going on, you've just essentially
declared yourself to be a full adult. I can't ground
you or even convince you to change your mind at
this point, so telling me more will probably just
make me worry even more than I already am."

I wasn't one of those kids who hated their
parents, in fact, my dad and I had always gotten
along pretty well, but that didn't mean that I
hadn't fantasized from time to time about being
on my own. Now that I'd arrived at that point, I
suddenly wished that there was a way to take
everything back and have my dad make all of
my decisions again.

There wasn't though, at least not a way that
also let me find out what was going on with
Caine and Jerek.

"Okay, Dad. Is there anything else?"

"Can you please ask your friend to let me go back home? My sitting here in the middle of nowhere stewing isn't going to do anything to keep you safe, so I'd just as soon be back home making sure that I still have a job."

"I don't think that's necessarily a very good idea, Dad. There are things...well, it's just not entirely safe back home right now. In a few days maybe things will be different, but until then..."

"No, Dani, I don't think so. You can't go off into danger and expect me not to do the same. I at least have a few extra decades of experience and am not directly caught up in whatever it is that you're so worried about. I'll be fine."

He was right. My wanting him to be safe while I traveled into who knew what kind of danger was the worst kind of hypocrisy, but that didn't stop me from looking for a way to stop from having to worry about him.

"And what happens if I don't ask Caine to let you go back home?"

"Then you will have lost my respect, Dani. I will still love you, but I won't trust you the way that I did before this. If you want to be treated like a responsible adult, then you need to treat me the same way."

I handed the phone back to Caine one last time. "Go ahead and do it."

"Are you sure this is a good idea?"

"No, but I don't have any other choice."

Caine pressed the receiver up tight against his chest to muffle our conversation. "I could just wipe your dad's memory, compel him to forget everything that's happened during the last twenty-four hours or so. I don't normally condone that kind of thing for anything less than preserving my race's secrets, but maybe this is one of those times…"

"No. Maybe you and Jerek can do that kind of thing and not turn into someone you'd rather not be, but I don't think I can. If I started down that path it would only be a matter of time until I was covering up even worse things, and I'm not sure I'm smart enough to make something like that stick. My dad would notice the bits and pieces that didn't add up. Credit card charges at gas stations he didn't remember going to would only be the start of what he would dig up once he really got started."

Caine nodded and then put the phone back up next to his ear. "You're free to go wherever you want, Mr. Destone."

Dad and I said our goodbyes and then it was just Caine, me, and Jerek's still form.

By that point both my emotions and thoughts were such a tangled mess that my curiosity was almost overpowered, but after a couple of minutes of silence I turned back to Caine.

"Are you at least going to tell me what the two of you are?"

"Sure, that's easy. We're gargoyles."

Chapter 8

"Did you really just say that you and Jerek are gargoyles? Do you have any idea how badly I want to freak out right now? Couldn't you have thought of an easier way to break this to me?"

Caine had the grace to look abashed. "Probably. I think that in your place I wouldn't be handling things anywhere close to as well as you've been handling them. I'm sorry, I wanted to tell you what was going on before I nodded off, but the venom was doing a real number on my system and I had a lot of injuries that made it even more critical for me to drop into a healing trance as quickly as possible. I really do wish that all of this could have gone down much differently than it has."

"Me too. Then again, it's not like it's really your fault. So, given that the two of you are...gargoyles, what exactly have I gotten myself into this time?"

"Well, you just wandered into the middle of a war that's been going on for longer than there's been recorded history."

"What kind of war?"

Caine shrugged. "I don't know, the kind where people die and innocents get caught up in tragic ways. The hunters aren't from Earth. They come from somewhere else, and there are only a few places where they can move from their home to ours. They use the portals to come here and feed on humans, while we guard the portals in an effort to keep as many of you as possible alive."

"Seriously? The fate of the world rests in the hands of two seventeen-year-olds?"

Caine pantomimed being stabbed in the chest. "You have no idea how much your words wound me. You would never say that if you had any idea how much I give up in order to fulfill my appointed task."

He managed to hold a serious expression for all of two seconds before starting to laugh. I shook my head at him in mock severity, but the truth was it was a relief to see him back to being his normal joking self. Crazy supernatural war or not, things couldn't be all that bad if Caine was still able to crack jokes.

"Oh, yes, great sacrifices. That's what I thought of when I first saw you at school. I said to myself, 'Self, that poor boy is really sacrificing a lot. He's been forced to drive a shiny car, wear nice clothes, and given the ability to woo any and all women he comes across.' I just don't know how you manage it, Caine."

Caine nodded earnestly. "I'm glad you're able to understand the cross I bear. You'd be amazed at how many people aren't able to comprehend my burdens."

I reached over and punched him in the arm, but without any real force since I didn't want to break any of the bones in my hands. "Okay, now that we've gotten that out of the way, how about you actually tell me something important."

"Okay, but it would sure be a lot more fun to spend the rest of the drive flirting with you."

I instantly blushed, but I knew from past experience not to take Caine too seriously. He waited a couple of seconds to see if I was going to provide more fodder for his teasing and then shrugged.

"Like I said, the hunters come to our world so they can feed off of the humans, but they can only do that in certain places. We call them portals. They are always underwater, and nobody from our world has ever gone through one and come back to tell us what's on the other side."

"So what, there's a portal in Lake Superior?"

"Ding, ding, we've got a winner here, give the girl her prize." Caine's response was said with all of his accustomed levity, but his face didn't match his words anymore. We were entering into the territory that even Caine took seriously.

"Time and time again, they appear without warning from one or more of the portals. They try to snatch people to take back to the other side, and we try to stop them, but there are a lot more of them than there are of us."

"And you guys are really gargoyles?"

"Yeah, at least that's the legend that matches up most closely with our abilities."

"So I know you have harder than normal skin. You're also crazy heavy, and apparently you guys really can sort of fly, but what else should I know about your species?"

"Yeah, you've pretty much identified the key elements that we are born with. There's a reason that all of those Gothic churches included stone statues around the roof. We used to cooperate very closely with the church back then, and that was a kind of code. Find a building with a gargoyle on it, and you could leave us messages if you knew how. The priests and monks used to call us the stone soldiers because we can make our skin hard enough to stop the hunters from piercing it."

"So you're not really made out of stone then? I mean, I touched your shoulder while you were asleep and you felt like you really were made out of rock."

I would have expected Caine to wiggle his eyebrows suggestively, but apparently he was still in a serious mood. "I don't really know, Dani. I can bleed, and I need to breathe, but you're right—when we go into a healing trance we basically turn into living statues. Maybe with the recent advances in the field of genetics someone will eventually figure out how exactly we do what we do, but for now, all I can tell you is we aren't human.

"Our night vision is really good, and we're stronger than humans, but that's just the tip of the iceberg. Like you noticed, we have a much greater body mass—and density—so swimming is basically out. We gargoyles sink like rocks, which may be why the hunters have chosen to locate all of their portals underwater where we can't get at them."

My mind was whirling as I tried to put together all of the information that he'd shared with me so far and slot it into the view of the world that I'd had growing up. I opened my mouth, intending on asking him more about their attributes, but then I realized that he hadn't been entirely truthful with me earlier.

"Wait a second, you told me that the people we were leaving back at the lake would be fine."

"Yeah, I told you that because they will be."

"No, you just finished telling me that the hunters take humans back to their dimension, or planet, or whatever. That means the people we left behind are very much not safe!"

My voice was getting louder with every word out of my mouth, but Caine was singularly unperturbed. "This conversation is going to take a lot longer if you interrupt me at every turn by jumping to conclusions, Dani. I haven't lied to you before now, and I'm not about to start. You have no idea how refreshing it was to find a girl I could talk to in Clay, Wisconsin.

"I stand by both of my statements. As of right now, everyone in Clay and the surrounding area is completely safe. Eventually, if we don't respond to the presence of hunters on Madeline Island, they are going to get more aggressive and start bringing people back to their portal, but we have some time before that will happen. Your dad, and everyone else back there will be just fine—I promise. The hunters need to feed in order to get their strength up to the point where they can bring in one of their elders. Until that happens, all of those lovely, two-legged food sources that you and I know and love aren't going anywhere."

"I know that you're trying to be reassuring, but I'm starting to wish I'd taken your suggestion and had you wipe my dad's memories so that we could keep him away from ground zero. By the way, it still kind of blows my mind that you can compel people over the phone like that."

"Yeah. It's harder to do compulsion like that from a long ways away, but that happens to be one of my specialties. I'll wait until school starts again tomorrow morning and then I'll call in to the office and get all three of us excused. It'll be like you never even missed any class—once we're back, I can even make it so you don't have to turn in make-up work if you're feeling particularly lazy."

I shook my head in amazement. "That's how you're keeping all of this a secret, isn't it? When that thing attacked Jerek and me at his house, I kept thinking that none of this could be real. I kept telling myself if those things were anything other than my imagination that they would be all over the news, but you guys are actively suppressing the news in order to keep your existence a secret, aren't you?"

"Yeah, basically. We have people in every major news organization and in all of the governments around the world who've been compelled to give our people a call if any word of the existence of the hunters shows up. Once we know who's got the relevant information, it's a small matter to get a hold of them and compel them to suppress it. I guess you could say all the conspiracy theorists are right—they just have the wrong conspiracy."

"So how come there's just you and Jerek there in Clay if your people know that at any moment the portal there could open up and start spewing out thousands of bloodthirsty hunters?"

"That's just the thing, that particular portal has been dormant for a really long time, so there wasn't a lot of reason to think that we were going to end up with that kind of activity out of nowhere. Usually when the hunters decide to reactivate a portal, they just send in one or two hunters to start preparing the way for more of their kind. All indications are that they are just as keen to keep their existence a secret as we are, so sending in a smaller force makes it easier for them to remain unseen until after the advance team has had a chance to start compelling a group of humans to help keep them off of our radar.

"There's a lot more of them than there are of us, so we've gone into the habit of leaving a single gargoyle in the neighborhood of any inactive portals so that we've got a tripwire if the hunters start trying to reactivate it. It's not a perfect system—sometimes the gargoyle who's supposed to be watching the area gets killed—but it's always worked pretty well, at least as far as making sure that we didn't get blindsided by a massive incursion. At least that's been the case until today."

"What do you mean? Isn't that exactly what happened today? They sent in a small team of three hunters and you and Jerek stopped them. Now you just need to call up your head commander or whoever and tell them to send in the cavalry so you can shut down the big incursion before it gets started."

Caine shook his head. "It's not quite that easy. Normally we can smell the hunters from miles away, so it's actually pretty rare for them to take us by surprise like that unless we've been sleeping or injured somehow and are in a healing trance. Those hunters back there, though, were completely scentless. That means we have no way of knowing how many of them there are in the area."

I was finally starting to understand what he was telling me. "So you're saying that the three you fought might not be the only three? They might be part of a much bigger group that's already come through the portal?"

"Yeah, that's what I'm worried about. The odds of that happening are astronomically against it, but this is the first time we've ever encountered a group of hunters who are able to sneak up on us like that. It's got me worrying that other things we've always taken as a given might be changing as well."

"So does that mean that my dad's not really safe? I mean, you just got done telling me that you don't actually know how far along this particular incursion is."

"No. I may be nervous about how many hunters we've got in the area, but I'm absolutely positive that we don't have an elder on our side of the portal yet. The elders are incredibly risk-averse and only come through when they've got hundreds of hunters in our world to protect them. If that were the case, they wouldn't have ambushed us with just three of their kind. They would've come after us with dozens so they could make sure we wouldn't be able to escape.

"Your dad is still safe; I'm just worried about what this might mean for the broader war. If the hunters are able to defeat our sense of smell, then there won't be anything to stop them from sneaking through our lines somewhere in the Middle East or in continental Africa and creating a new stronghold somewhere we're not expecting it."

"So there's fighting going on all the time?"

Caine nodded. "Yeah, if there's one constant to life, it's the fact that somewhere on our planet there is a major incursion going on. Basically, you can point to anywhere where lots of people are being killed and it's a pretty good bet that the root cause is a big group of hunters who are trying to expand their foothold on our world. Generally speaking, by the time they're ready to bring an elder through they'll have started a war or two in their immediate area to serve as additional cover against us. Wherever possible, we try not to kill innocent humans, and when there's a war going on, it gets a lot harder to pick out who is innocent and who isn't."

"So are you guys winning?"

"That depends on who you believe. The incursions we're fighting right now have been going on for a very long time, and it doesn't seem to matter how many of them we kill, there are still more of them showing up every day. If something doesn't change soon I'm afraid that our losses are going to start catching up with us."

I shook myself slightly, trying to pull back from the vision of death and destruction that Caine's words were conjuring inside of my mind, and pulled my phone back out of my pocket. "It sounds like you probably better use this to round up some reinforcements, then. If this is the beginning of another incursion it would be a heck of a lot better to nip it in the bud now than let it get big enough that they start preparing to bring in one of their elders."

Caine grimaced. "Yeah, I've been thinking the same thing, but Jerek was adamant about choosing the timing of this particular call. He seems to think that it's best if we don't call in until we're too close to Salt Lake for them to just order us back to Wisconsin. If Jerek says that's the way to go, then that's what we'll do—he's the boss."

"Why Jerek? Aren't you both stationed there with the responsibility of keeping an eye on the portal?"

"Yeah, but things are probably going to go a lot better if it's Jerek who reaches out to our leaders to ask for reinforcements."

I felt like I was having to pull teeth to get a straight answer out of Caine, so I fixed him with a stern look and cocked my head to one side.

"And why exactly is that, Caine?"

"Jerek's mom doesn't really like me. Actually, that's part of why I was out there instead of being assigned a more important job."

"I still don't get it. What does Jerek's mom have to do with anything? Who is she exactly?"

"The queen of the gargoyles, and defender of the faith, long may she live. I'm guessing it didn't come up in your earlier conversation with Jerek that he's the crown prince of an entire supernatural race?"

Chapter 9

Caine's revelation about Jerek was such a shock that it pretty much killed the conversation between us for the next hour or so. A few minutes later, Caine pulled over for gas—which I had to pump given that I was the only one who wasn't wearing bloody, shredded clothes.

Once we were back on the road, and once again driving in relative silence, I finally noticed just how fast Caine was driving. I would have told him he was asking to have his license revoked, but it was pretty obvious that he wasn't worried about getting pulled over by a cop.

Apparently traffic laws were little more than sensible suggestions when you were capable of stopping cops from pulling you over with little more than a thought or two. As he cranked the speed of the SUV up into triple digits I found myself gripping onto my seat in much the same fashion as I had on the boat earlier that day. Being told that the driver who held your life in his hand had superhuman reaction time was all well and good in theory, but that didn't change the fact that all it would take was a split-second of inattention on Caine's part to send the three of us careening into a fiery explosion.

As time wore on, I caught Caine looking at the clock on the dash more and more frequently and I could tell he was starting to feel the pressure to call Jerek's mother build with each passing minute. Fortunately, it was about that time when Jerek finally woke up and asked if he could use my cell phone. I passed it back to him and then listened to one half of a conversation that didn't make much sense to me, but which seemed to boil down to the fact that Jerek's mother would be meeting us in Salt Lake.

Trying to interpret what was being said on the other side of the conversation distracted me slightly from my budding terror at Caine's driving, but once Jerek hung up with his mother I felt my anxiety starting to build again. Surprisingly, only a minute or so after the end of his conversation with his mother, Jerek leaned forward to where he could see the speedometer and ordered Caine to slow down.

"Given flight times from the Holy Lands, and the estimate of when my mom's plane is going to be in the air, there's no reason for you to be speeding like that. I'll be able to get to Salt Lake in plenty of time to meet with my mother if you keep it to within five miles an hour of the speed limit."

Caine grumbled at the order, but apparently being crown prince meant that Jerek really did get to order people around pretty much at will. Caine slowed down to just over the speed limit and then did a double take.

"What do you mean *you* will get there in plenty of time?"

"The last thing I want is for Dani to be anywhere near my mother. You're thrilled that Dani is immune to compulsion, but Mother will take a very different view of that situation."

"She's going to view Dani as a security risk, isn't she?"

"Very much so. A human who can't be compelled is a human who can't be controlled, but knowing the way my mother's mind works, that's only the beginning of the concerns she'll have regarding Dani."

It was my turn to jump into the conversation. "What do you mean by that?"

Jerek looked over at me and stared for a couple of seconds—obviously choosing his words with care—before responding.

"Our people have remained a secret for thousands of years precisely because we can make humans unable to talk about us, or in extreme circumstances even make them forget about our existence altogether. Mother will worry that your resistance to compulsion is some kind of evolutionary mutation that could be passed on to any children you might have."

"And that would be a bad thing?"

"In her mind? Yes."

I still had a lot of residual anger floating around inside of me from what Jerek had pretended to do earlier, but there was something in his voice that cut through all of that.

"You don't sound like you're quite so sure about that."

"I'm not. From a strictly big-picture angle, the biggest reason humans have traditionally been kept in the dark is that their susceptibility to compulsion—both ours and the cruder version used by the hunters—makes them unable to fight against the hunters. You weren't completely immune to the hunter we fought back on Madeline Island, but you were resistant enough to open up new possibilities when it comes to cooperation between your people and mine."

"You mean like humans fighting side by side with gargoyles?"

"In a perfect world that would be the case, but there are other possible benefits as well. Even if a significant percentage of the humans out there aren't resistant enough to fight, just having humans able to alert us when an incursion started would be a tremendous help."

Jerek paused again. "As important as that could be for the war effort, on a personal level, I just really want you to be able to make your own decisions. As I told you back at the house, Mother is so sure of the righteousness of her cause that she'll do almost anything in its service."

"Define *anything*."

"She would detain you in Salt Lake out of nothing more than reflex, of that much I am certain. Beyond that, I suspect that you would be subjected to a full battery of genetic tests—including harvesting genetic material so that additional tests could be run on your code as the field of genetics advances. You could expect to be subject to all manner of other experiments designed to ascertain the limits of your abilities, and only then after all of the data is in—which could easily take years—would my mother actually decide what to do with you on a long-term basis."

My face felt like a wooden mask. I was so horrified by what he was describing that I couldn't get any of my muscles to respond to the signals desperately racing outward from my brain. Jerek gave me a sad smile.

"That is why the plan has always been to part ways well before we make it back to Salt Lake. You and Caine can purchase a vehicle and head somewhere safe while I deal with my mother."

Caine frowned. "You do realize that my not being there when you talk to the queen could be viewed as a form of desertion, right?"

"Yeah, but I think I can smooth that over with Mother, especially if you are headed back in the general direction of Wisconsin while I'm talking to her. It's a pretty simple story to spin. You and I were injured, one of the girls from the party drove us westward until we were both healed, and then you and I parted ways so that you could go back and monitor the situation. You're just going to want to make sure that you time things so that you don't actually make it back there until I land with reinforcements."

It sounded like a decent plan to me, but Caine's nod was a lot more hesitant than I was used to seeing out of him. I had a feeling I wasn't really going to want to know the reason why, but I was starting to realize just how deep the waters I was trying to swim in really were. If I was going to have any chance of charting my own course through what was coming toward me, then I needed to know as much as possible about this new world I'd stumbled into.

"You don't seem convinced, Caine."

He shrugged. "It's a good plan—Jerek has obviously given this a ton more thought than I have. I never got past just thinking it was cool that you could push past compulsion."

"But?"

"But his mother is relentless. It's a bit like what you were worried about with your dad when I proposed wiping his memory. Whenever we try to alter reality there a chance that someone will worry at the stuff that doesn't add up until they either figure out their memories have been altered, or they ended up checked into a mental hospital somewhere. This isn't really all that different than that. Jerek knows about you, I know about you, and I'm worried that one of us will let something slip that will make the queen realize we're keeping something from her."

I looked over at Jerek expectantly and he nodded. "Mother has resources at her disposal that most people can't even imagine. It goes beyond just Caine and me. If she decides that there is a secret worth knowing surrounding the events yesterday, it's not at all beyond her to send a squad of her best troubleshooters to interrogate the rest of the kids at the party. Forewarned is forearmed, and Caine is one of the best when it comes to compulsion, but he's not actually *the* best."

"Thanks, buddy."

"Sorry, Caine, but you know it's true, and you know that if Mother really thinks we are keeping something important from her she'll send one of the few people who can reliably break your compulsion. At that point, it will become very obvious to her investigators that Dani wasn't reacting the way that a normal human would have."

Caine nodded sourly. "You'll pardon me for saying it, but your mom can be a real bi—"

"Caine!"

He had the grace to look embarrassed, which was almost as surprising as the fact that I'd objected to him insulting a woman who sounded like she was fully capable of killing me.

"Sorry, but it's true."

Jerek nodded. "A lot worse has been said of her in the past, and being her son hasn't made me incapable of seeing her faults."

Caine ran his hand through his hair and sighed. "So then what? I've known you for long enough to realize that you've already started prepping a contingency plan for your contingency plan."

"If Mother finds out about Dani, then our only other real option would be to send Dani and her father into hiding."

"Wait, you mean like witness protection?"

"Yes, that's right. I've got sufficient funds to ensure that the two of you will be able to start a new life somewhere completely off the radar."

"Meaning Dad and I will spend the rest of our lives looking over our shoulders?"

"That is an unfortunate side effect of living on the run."

Under any other circumstances I would have been confident that Jerek and Caine were pranking me, but after everything I'd seen since arriving in Wisconsin, there was no doubt in my mind that they were telling the truth.

I reached for an alternative plan, and instead just kept coming up with more problems with Jerek's plan.

"I think you're trying to cushion the blow. If your mom is really as sneaky and tenacious as you're implying, then sending me back home to try to live a normal life for as long as possible just means that when she sends people for me, they will come when I least expect it. If I really want to be safe then I would need to go on the run immediately."

Caine closed his eyes as though wishing he could refute my logic, and when he spoke it was almost as though the words were being dragged out of him by force.

"She's not wrong."

"I want another option then. Caine said you have backup plans to your backups, what was option number two?"

"It's less likely to succeed…"

"I want to hear it anyway."

"As much as she might wish otherwise, Mother is not the supreme ruler of the universe. Even she has to bow to popular pressures from time to time, and she can only ferret out secrets once she realizes that there is something to go looking for. Instead of trying to keep our secret in the sneaky way that is most people's first instinct, we take the opposite approach. Dani goes in to the audience with us, and we make her an object of admiration among as many of our kind as we can expose her to."

Jerek was looking less and less happy by the minute about what he was proposing, but he kept talking regardless and I was starting to suspect that there was a stubborn core of honesty to him that disapproved of his actions earlier nearly as much as I disapproved.

"We play up the fact that she helped us of her own free will, and spread that information as far and wide as we can."

"Only I didn't help you of my own free will, you tricked me and threatened people I care about."

"Exactly. Mother will sense that there is something off with our story and she'll spend her efforts trying to prove that there is no way that a human could have done the things we're claiming you did. Confirmation bias among her and her people should buy us a period of time in which they don't realize the secret we are actually hiding is much more important than she realizes."

"You're talking about hiding her in plain sight, and then hoping that by the time the queen realizes what's really going on it will be too late to treat her like a science experiment without making the nobility revolt."

"Indeed."

"Is that even possible?"

Jerek nodded. "It's been done before, but never with a secret this big—not without a ton more lead up than we would have. My suggestion is still to take the first option; it has the best chance of succeeding."

I looked back and forth between the two of them, wishing that there was an easy answer, wishing that I could just delegate the decision to someone else, but my dad had been right. In choosing to disobey him and stay with Jerek and

Caine I'd declared myself an adult, and adults didn't just get to pass on the hard decisions. Anyone who just spoke up for the easy choices and never decided when things got hard wasn't an adult, they were just a kid playing at being an adult. I wanted to be an adult.

"You're right, the first plan has the best chance of succeeding, but even success isn't all that great of an achievement. I don't want to spend the rest of my life on the run, keeping secrets from everyone around me. I know that my curse may make forming any kind of real relationship impossible, but if it does happen I want to be able to tell whoever I end up with the truth.

"What do you think, Caine? Can Jerek really pull off the second option?"

"I don't know that anyone is capable of double- and triple-thinking the queen like that, but if it's possible, Jerek is the guy to do it."

Jerek had been so calm when laying out the options that it took me completely by surprise when he scowled. It didn't make any sense, but all I could figure was that he didn't like me getting a second opinion from Caine.

"So that's it? Just like that it's settled? What if I don't want to take on the task of making you the darling of the nobility?"

"Well, then I guess you could just tell your mother the truth and let the chips fall where they may."

"I could make you take the first option."

"Really? How are you going to do that? You can't compel me and if you send me off by myself I don't have to make a run for it, I can just go back home and do something stupid enough to attract your mother's attention."

"I could send Caine with you."

That actually made me laugh. "I don't think Caine is going to obey that particular order, and even if he did, you and I both know that unless he's going to keep me tied up twenty-four hours a day, eventually I'll manage to get away."

Jerek opened his mouth as though about to give me a piece of his mind, but I beat him to the punch.

"Most importantly though, *making* me do anything doesn't jive with you wanting to make sure that I get the chance to make my own decisions."

That pulled him up short. "You're right. I wouldn't have actually tried to make you take option number one. If you want to try hiding in plain sight then that's what we'll try to do. I just really don't want to see you become a captive or have something even worse happen to you."

"Why? We've known each other less than a day—why do you care?"

"Let's just say that I have a pretty good idea what you're capable of becoming, Dani. I'd really hate to see you lose out on that."

Chapter 10

The next several hours disappeared in a blur of moving vistas, restless sleep inside of a moving vehicle, and short stops at gas stations to grab food and use the bathroom.

Caine and Jerek did almost all of the driving—although I did get another shift around midmorning—which left me with a lot of time on my hands. I had a lot more questions for Caine about what it was like to be a gargoyle and the current state of the war, but I just couldn't seem to bring myself to ask any of them with Jerek around.

I didn't hate Jerek anymore, but beyond that my feelings were a tangled mess. Once I'd asserted my right to choose my own fate, he'd retreated back behind the facade of cool, mostly-polite indifference that had characterized our interactions back at the island before the attack, which meant I had next to nothing to go on with regards to where I stood with him.

Caine made a valiant attempt to engage both Jerek and me in conversation at various points during the trip, but I was still too self-conscious around Jerek to let Caine pull me into our normal easy banter, and Jerek was too absorbed in his thoughts to pay either of us much attention.

Despite Jerek's order to keep the speed limit down to something more reasonable, we rolled into Salt Lake in record time the next day, and shortly after that pulled up to a house—set against the side of a mountain—that made the mansion back on Madeline Island look like a poorly constructed children's treehouse. I should have realized that would be the case, given that Madeline Island was a secondary portal which wasn't important enough to station more than two guards at, but I was still trying to understand just how different the world Jerek lived in was than the one in which I'd grown up.

He wasn't just rich the way that oil tycoons or dotcom billionaires were rich, he was rich the way that European royal families were rich. I had very little doubt but that his family was capable of buying and selling small countries out of nothing more than their petty cash fund, and I found myself wondering what it must have been like to grow up knowing that money was never going to be a concern.

Once I got past the obvious splendor of the exterior of Jerek's house, I started to realize that it wasn't just a home. The carefully manicured grounds, complete with sculptures, fountains, and the biggest hedge maze I'd ever seen, were designed to look like nothing more than the estate of some massively wealthy family, but as we pulled into a gigantic underground parking garage that was only half full of exotic sports cars and expensive black SUVs, I started to realize that Jerek's home was also the capital and administrative center for an entire supernatural nation.

That realization was reinforced as I was conducted upward from the garage into the lower levels. There was security, much of it passive and all of it unobtrusive, at nearly every turn. We passed more than a dozen men in suits who I was pretty sure were packing guns of some kind or another underneath those expensively tailored jackets, and at one point as we came around a corner, I saw someone leaving a room that looked like some kind of armory from out of a military base.

There were black rifles and deadly-looking submachine guns hanging from the wall, and enough ammunition to blow up a big chunk of the house if it ever caught fire squirreled away in the metal containers that I'd seen on some of the prepper shows that Sally was so fond of back when I'd lived in Utah.

The thought of Sally made me wish that I could talk to her about everything that had happened since I'd arrived in Clay, but I knew that would be a really bad idea. I was having a hard enough time believing it all and I'd seen the proof with my own eyes. If I told Sally that the world was under attack by sickly white monsters from another dimension, the best-case scenario would be that she would think I was joking. It would be far more likely that she would decide I was crazy and needed some kind of therapy.

The realization that I was even more different from the rest of the people out there in the normal world was more than a little depressing, but even that couldn't distract me from the fact that Jerek's home had a lot more in common with the White House in Washington, DC than it did with my house.

As we got to the top of the third flight of stairs, I looked up to find that Jerek was deep in conversation with an older man in a butler's uniform. The fact that he was so distracted was the only reason I was able to bring myself to start asking Caine questions again.

"Are all of these people like you? I thought you said there weren't very many gargoyles."

I'd been expecting Caine to laugh, or at least tease me a little, but apparently the prospect of being in the presence of a queen who didn't like him had sobered even Caine's normally un-quenchable sense of humor. He double-checked that nobody was close enough to overhear us and then shook his head.

"No, they're humans like you—well, not exactly like you. I don't remember ever hearing about anyone else able to completely shrug off our compulsion, so it appears that you're unique. In fact, if these people were like you they would be the last individuals Jerek's family would want working here at the estate."

"You guys have them all compelled, don't you?" I couldn't help it, my question came out much louder than Caine's explanation. Not the thing to do if I was trying to maintain a low profile.

Jerek turned back and gave the two of us a frown. "Yes, everyone here who's not a gargoyle has been compelled to be loyal and never mention any word of what takes place inside these walls to anyone. It's an unfortunate operational necessity, but we make sure that all of our people are well taken care of. We pay salaries twenty percent above anyone else in the entire state, but if someone wants to leave we let them go with our blessing."

"After you wipe away all memories of working here?"

"Yes, after we destroy any memories that could come back to cause us problems in the future. As long as they are here at the estate where we can monitor them, it's a simple matter to make sure that they don't fall under the sway of the hunters, but once they express a desire to leave it becomes unfeasible for us to monitor them around the clock to make sure that they won't leak our existence under orders from one of the hunters."

Normally I was too timid to court the kind of confrontation I was flirting with now, but something about the plight of Jerek's employees had struck a chord inside of me. Maybe it was just the fact that I could've easily been in their shoes if not for my unusual immunity to gargoyle powers of persuasion. It was hard to look at other people being treated as no more than playthings when you knew it could've easily been you instead.

"Do you really think that paying them a little bit extra makes up for the fact that you've taken away their free will?"

Jerek flinched, but his response came back without any other sign that I'd struck home with my last comment.

"You're making judgments about things you're not prepared to understand, Dani. As I just finished saying, each and every employee of the estate has the option of leaving our employment at any time. Even before they are compelled for the first time, they sign a release allowing us to remove their memories from their time working here in the event they leave. It's all very aboveboard, and legal."

"Really? They sign a piece of paper saying that you'll destroy their memories in the event that they get fired?"

"Not in quite so many words, but non-disclosure agreements are very common in this day and age."

I turned to the butler who'd been watching our exchange impassively. "How do you feel about all of this? Do you really have a choice?"

"Indeed, miss, I do. It was my choice to enter into this employment, and should I desire to leave the employ of the Hammerfell family, I may do so at any time."

"But you're not going to, are you?"

"No, miss, I'm not. Contrary to what you appear to believe, those of us who work here at the estate are fully briefed on the unusual nature of our employers once we sign on. I may not have the skill set with which to fight the hunters with my bare hands, but by ensuring the smooth operation of this house, I help assist those who can. I feel it is not unreasonable to say that in my own way I am playing a vital role in saving the human race. Right or wrong, I feel that no sacrifice made to bring about that end is un-reasonable."

Chapter 11

There wasn't a lot I could say after a statement like that. It was obvious that Jerek's butler was a true believer, in every sense of the word, and I didn't know enough about the rest of the situation to feel comfortable getting into an argument with him.

I quietly followed Jerek and Caine as we were led to a suite of rooms on the second floor and told that we could refresh ourselves while we waited for the queen to arrive. Caine followed me into my room and showed me a closet full of clothes in various colors, styles and sizes that he said I was welcome to change into once I finished showering.

The more I thought about it, the better taking a shower sounded. Jerek's mom might not be the ruler of my particular country, but I was pretty sure she wasn't used to entertaining guests who were wearing nothing more than a T-shirt and some board shorts over a bikini. I showed Caine out, locked the door behind him, and then took the fastest shower of my existence because I was so worried that she would arrive before I was done, and I would start things out on the wrong foot with her as a result.

I exited the shower, pink from all of the scrubbing, only to realize that my problems were just starting. I had no idea what one wore to an audience with the queen of the gargoyles, but slipping back on my old, dirty clothes would defeat the point of showering in the first place. I wrapped a towel around myself and then stepped out into the main common area, hoping I'd be able to find Caine and ask him for advice before I ran into anyone else. I should've known that my luck wasn't that good.

Caine was nowhere in sight, but Jerek was pacing back and forth across the room. He looked up as I stepped out, and arched his eyebrow in an inquiring look.

"Problems, Dani?"

My face instantly heated up, and I had to fight the urge to retreat back into my room. I was nearly as covered as I'd been when I'd arrived at Jerek's mansion in Wisconsin, but there was something unquestionably different about being around a guy wearing nothing more than a towel.

"Yeah, I was hoping I could find Caine so he could explain what kind of outfit I should be wearing to the audience with your mother."

Jerek studied me for several seconds before shaking his head. "I'm sorry, but that's a terrible idea. Caine is the worst when it comes to these types of things—it's part of why my mother hates him. Come on, I'll help you pick out something suitable."

Jerek stepped past me heading into my room without waiting to see if I was going to follow him. I was tempted to run the other direction, but I knew that would be absurd. It wasn't like I would get very far in nothing more than the towel, but I was suddenly uncomfortable with the idea of being alone inside a bedroom with Jerek once again.

I took a deep breath and then turned and followed him into the room. He already had a number of articles of clothing spread across the bed, mostly combinations of blue and black. He looked up at me as I entered the room, and then nodded at the dresser located in one corner of the walk-in closet.

"These rooms are used for short-term visitors, so they're stocked with everything you could need over the course of several days. My parents often entertain people who travel at short notice without most of the normal preparations, so our situation is a lot less uncommon than you might think. There's a variety of brand-new, freshly laundered underwear in that drawer, but if you are unable to find anything suitable I can take your measurements to one of the maids and have her dig something up that will fit better."

By the time Jerek finished speaking, he'd already turned back to the hangers full of clothes, but that didn't make me feel any less self-conscious as I walked over to the dresser and pulled open the top drawer. I would've said that picking out underwear around any guy would've been incredibly embarrassing, but I wasn't sure that was really the case.

If it had been Caine in the room with me, he would've said something flirtatious that would've made me roll my eyes and then I would've sent him out of the room until I'd picked out the necessary articles of clothing to go underneath the outfits Jerek was laying out on the bed, but I didn't feel like I could kick Jerek out of the room so soon after asking him for help.

I told myself that it wasn't as if he was expecting me to model the underwear for him and forced myself to start looking for something in my size. Everything was laid out very logically by size moving from left to right, and it took me only a few seconds to find both a bra and panties that would work until I could return home and go back to wearing my own clothes.

Everything in the dresser had been very utilitarian, and white cotton wasn't typically considered to be the height of sexy, but I was blushing once again as I pulled the undergarments out of the drawers and hid them behind my back.

I knew Jerek had seen me turn an even brighter shade of red, but he was surprisingly gentlemanly about it.

That, or he was just completely uninterested. I was fairly sure it was the latter, but I tried to tell myself that what I was feeling was most definitely not disappointment.

"During my grandparents' time the court was much more traditional, but my father decreed that all of the pomp and pageantry was a waste of resources that were better spent combating the hunters, so you should be fine in any of the outfits I've placed on the bed. I'll leave now so you can change, but if you have any problems just call out. I'll be within earshot."

I was pretty sure that my voice wasn't going to work right then, so I just nodded wordlessly and waited as Jerek pulled the door shut behind him. It took me only a few moments to try on the top outfit, and I instantly knew I wasn't going to bother with any of the rest.

Jerek had picked out black dress pants that were surprisingly flattering for something I would've expected to see on a bank teller, and a light blue dress shirt that fit better than anything I had back in my closet at home. I surveyed the results in the long mirror in the bathroom, put on some black pumps, and then grabbed my phone and walked out to the common area again.

Jerek had been joined by Caine, who likewise looked freshly showered, and who was wearing khaki slacks and a very stylish dress shirt of his own. Caine let out a low whistle as I entered the room.

"Looking good, Dani. I knew you were hot stuff, but I didn't expect you to come out looking like that."

I instantly started to panic, and looked back and forth between Jerek and Caine. Caine was dressed in the same kind of clothes as I had on, but Jerek was wearing cargo pants and a T-shirt that was tight enough I could see his muscles bulging underneath it.

"Why, is this not what I should be wearing?"

I nearly started hyperventilating at that point, but Jerek responded before Caine could get a word out. "You look perfect, Dani. I promise I didn't steer you wrong—Caine didn't pick out his ensemble either. After a particularly dreadful encounter between him and my mother two years ago, I picked out three different sets of clothing that I knew would be stocked at either capital, and told him he wasn't allowed to wear anything other than those while he was here."

"What about you? You look decidedly like the odd man out."

Jerek shrugged. "As the heir, I get more latitude than Caine does. Mother won't like the way I'm dressed, but if she chooses to complain about that, it will just mean that she's not complaining about something that actually matters."

He was obviously referencing our plan to try and keep his mother off balance about my capabilities—only I got the feeling that there was more to it than that. Unfortunately, before I could ask for clarification, one of the footmen knocked on the door to our suite and then let himself in.

"I'm sorry to interrupt, sir, but the queen has arrived at the estate. She's asked for you to meet her in her study."

Jerek nodded his thanks, and then gestured for Caine and me to follow him. Before either of us could take a step forward, the footman cleared his throat. "Her Royal Grace was very specific. She asked to see you alone."

Jerek gave the poor employee a cold smile as he picked up a small black bag that I hadn't noticed sitting on the couch behind him. Caine had a similar bag, but before I could start worrying that I'd done something wrong by not getting a bag of my own, Jerek pointed at my room.

"Please see to it that Dani's things are gathered up and waiting for us just outside of Mother's study. I don't anticipate there will be time for the three of us to come back here before we leave."

The footman cleared his throat nervously. "My apologies, sir. I fear that I have done a poor job communicating. Her Royal Highness has expressed a desire to talk to you alone. Your friends will be taken care of here in your suite."

"Yes, I'm sure my mother expressed that desire to you—I'm sure she expresses many desires to any number of people throughout the course of any given day—but, fortunately for all of us, she is only a queen rather than the omnipotent ruler of the universe. Even queens sometimes benefit from not getting everything they want. You've done your job, and I will make sure my mother is aware of that fact, but Dani and Caine are coming with me."

Jerek walked out of the room without looking back at the footman, and Caine nudged me from behind to get me moving along in Jerek's wake. "Trust me when I say you're going to want to arrive right on Jerek's heels rather than twenty seconds later."

"Are you sure? Letting him and his mother square off against each other by themselves seems like the best idea I've heard in weeks."

"What, and leave our fearless leader all by himself? Perish the thought, milady."

I could hear the levity in Caine's voice—he'd made no attempt at hiding it—but it only did so much to reassure me. Still, it wasn't like I had a lot of other options, so I sped up to something only a hair slower than a run so as to make sure I didn't fall too far behind Jerek.

We headed through a bewildering array of twists and turns that I was sure would take me months to memorize, but Jerek's pace never slowed as he led us deeper and deeper into the mansion. After just five minutes of walking I was pretty sure we'd covered more distance than had been contained inside the house, and I began to suspect that we'd gone into the side of the mountain behind the estate. Apparently Jerek's family took security even more seriously than I'd realized.

The queen's study turned out to be nothing at all like I'd been expecting. I'd assumed that she would be receiving us in a scaled-up version of my dad's office inside our house, but instead what I found waiting for us was something that could only be described as a miniature throne room with bookcases along the walls and several imposing desks clustered behind the massive, throne-like seat his mother was sitting in.

"I see that you did not receive my message, Jerek. I instructed the footman to invite just you here. I suppose I'll have to see to it that Howard has that footman's pay docked for failing to convey my wishes."

The queen didn't rise from her seat, which didn't particularly surprise me given the obvious tension between her and Jerek, but since her attention was focused entirely on him I took the opportunity to study her. She was a powerful-looking woman in her late forties with piercing blue eyes and the same wavy hair that Jerek made look so devastatingly hand-some, albeit hers was down past her shoulders. She was also quite obviously pregnant, which was more than a little jarring given her apparent age.

"We both know that the footman did exactly as he was supposed to, Mother. If you're going to punish someone, punish me. I was the one who instructed my friends to accompany me into your presence. It seemed pointless to leave them behind when I knew that you would need to discuss the events in Wisconsin with them."

The queen's mouth tightened almost imperceptibly before she waved away Jerek's statement. "I think you're blowing this out of proportion, my son."

"Perhaps I was not paying as much attention to the royal tutors during my formative years as I should have, but it was my understanding that maintaining the safety of the realm was the single most important duty of the royal family. Given that, I have a hard time understanding how I could possibly be blowing a new hunter incursion out of proportion."

The queen shook her head and pointed at the lip ring on the right side of Jerek's mouth. "I can't believe you're not yet ready to get rid of that thing. It is woefully unbecoming of a prince of the realm. Your brother Harold would never dream of wearing something like that."

Jerek's fists went white, but other than that he betrayed no indication of how angry his mother's words were making him.

"If my appearance offends you so much, then you're free to make Harold the heir to the throne. I would happily step aside in his favor if that was what you and Father decided was best for the kingdom."

"You know very well that we can't do that. I imagine that's why you continue to be so defiant. Despite your neglect of the duties which traditionally fall to the crown prince, you continue to enjoy an unsettling amount of support among significant segments of the guard. If we were to pass you over in favor of Harold, it is entirely possible that the kingdom would experience a schism."

"As I said in the past, Mother, I'm more than happy to make whatever public statement is required to assure all of your loyal subjects that Harold has my full support."

The queen shook her head in frustration before turning her gaze to Caine and me. "I see that you're still associating with this wastrel despite my objections."

"Caine has never done anything but support the monarchy and fulfill his duty, Mother. You shame yourself in talking to him so, and if you don't show him the respect he is due, I will stop showing up for the state functions that mean so much to you."

"And her? Who is this human female you've brought into my presence without even bothering with proper introductions? Is this the reason you've refused all three of the candidates who were presented to you last year? Was it due to love for some human?"

STONE HEART

I found myself gritting my teeth to stop from saying something that would just make the situation worse, but fortunately Jerek seemed more than ready to defend me to his mother.

"I made no introductions simply because your rudeness prohibited the normal forms of politeness, Mother. Danielle Destone is due all of the respect you would normally accord any member of the guard, and I would appreciate you demonstrating said respect to her. If not for her help yesterday, neither Caine nor I would've survived to make it here to report on the growing infestation of hunters in Wisconsin."

The anger that had been bubbling under the surface of the queen's demeanor rose to the top and she slapped her hands down on the arms of her throne with such force that I expected something to break.

"I will not be spoken to in such a manner—not even by my own son. This is yet another in a long line of ridiculous demands. You can't really expect me to accord some floozy you coerced into providing transportation the same respect as the loyal members of the guard who risk their lives time and time again to keep both this world and this family safe."

Jerek opened his mouth to respond to his mother's accusations, but she was not done speaking, and the rapidly rising volume of her voice stopped him from getting a word in edgewise.

"I will not have it, Jerek. I want her out of this room this instant."

I took a step backwards fully intending on complying with her order, but Jerek motioned for me to stay, and for one terrible instant I was stuck trying to decide which order to obey. If she'd allowed me to make up my own mind, it was entirely possible that I would've chosen to bow out of their little family dispute, but when I didn't move quickly enough to satisfy her, Jerek's mother decided to take matters into her own hands.

Between one heartbeat and the next I felt pressure materialize inside my skull and realized that she was trying to force me to obey her order. The plan had called for me not to flaunt my immunity to compulsion, but Jerek once again motioned for me to stay put.

There was no way to know for sure that he understood she was using compulsion to force me out of the room, but somewhere along the way that stopped mattering. However much my natural disposition might be to give people the benefit of the doubt and back away from confrontation, I knew this was a defining moment. Backing down now would mean that I would always have to back down to her in the future—which wasn't particularly appealing—but even more than that, I was plain and simply tired of being pushed around. Jerek motioning for me to stay gave me the excuse I needed to stand my ground for the first time in what felt like forever.

I registered her attempt to bend me to her will, and simply allowed myself to ignore the growing impulse to turn and walk back the way I'd come. I raised my chin slightly and locked stares with her, completely forgetting for a moment that there was anyone else in the room.

Her expression could have frozen water from five yards away. "These little games stopped amusing me long ago, Jerek. Simply counteracting my compulsion with your own proves nothing but the fact that you are in open rebellion against your father and me."

"I'm afraid you have quite misunderstood the situation, Mother. I am not using compulsion on Dani any more than Caine is. Dani is a special kind of unique. She is completely immune to our compulsion, and even partially immune to the cruder, more brute-force method that the hunters use to control their prey.

"As I've been trying to tell you, Dani did not help us out of compulsion, but rather of her own free will. After our confrontation with the hunters—both on Madeline Island and on the mainland—Caine and I were severely wounded enough that we would not have been able to get to a safe distance from the scene of the battle before having to go into healing trances. If Dani had not agreed to come with us, it is entirely possible that Caine and I could've been killed while defenseless before our bodies finished repairing themselves. I must reiterate that Dani is due just as much respect as any member of your household."

The queen leaned back in her throne and gave me a considering look before allowing her compulsion to evaporate. There was a calculating feel to her expression as she turned back to her son.

"You're overstating the danger you were in, and we both know it. If Dani had not been there to drive you to safety, you still could've easily compelled someone else to do the task, but that is beside the point. Don't think that I haven't realized how carefully you avoided answering my question, Jerek. This girl is the reason that you've been refusing to bond any of the candidates who have been presented to you, isn't she? Are you so far gone as to think that you love her?"

Jerek's mom was losing points with every passing second, but the disdain with which she treated the idea of Jerek and me being together was somehow the worst part of it. I knew that Jerek wasn't interested in me and, my industrial-sized butterflies notwithstanding, I wasn't interested in him either. That didn't change the fact that it was insulting for her to treat me like I was nothing more than gutter trash.

Unfortunately, Jerek's response didn't make me feel any better. "Dani is Caine's friend, mother. I did not choose to bond any of the three candidates you presented me with this year simply because I no longer believe it to be right for our kind to enter into relationships with humans solely with the intent of bonding them."

"That's a lie, and you know it. I may not yet have been able to figure out exactly what it is you're lying about when you try to stand by those ancient traditions, but I know there is a falsehood there. Why won't you accept the legacy your ancestors worked so hard to provide you?"

Jerek looked back at me for half a second, and once again I was having a hard time interpreting the look on his face. I would've almost said he was sorry, but he hadn't said anything that he needed to apologize to me for, and the next thing out of his mouth didn't seem to have anything to do with me at all.

"My reasons are my own, Mother, but you will sense the truth of this statement. I have no desire to bond anyone you could possibly set before me. Bonding humans is a barbaric practice that comes at far too steep a price for everyone involved. I will not be part of destroying someone whose only crime is that of having lost some grand genetic lottery. Now, are we going to discuss the infestation of hunters in Wisconsin, or has the crown ceased to fulfill its primary responsibility?"

Jerek's mother looked like she wanted to pick up her throne and throw it at her son, but apparently even being queen didn't mean that she could indulge all of her impulses. She pressed a button on the arm of her throne and a second later the doors behind us opened up and a quartet of big, well-muscled guys walked in.

"I will, of course, see to the situation in Wisconsin. I'll have a squad of riven on their way back to your post within the hour. They will destroy whatever hunters might have slipped through the portal, and assess the likelihood of a larger incursion."

Jerek shook his head. "Four riven is not a large enough force. I would like for you to place an entire wing of troops under my command to scour the area. As I told you during our initial phone call, these hunters were unlike any I've ever encountered in the past. They had no scent, which means they're going to be much more difficult to track down than a normal group. If you send such a small force, it's entirely possible that they will be ambushed and destroyed if the incursion is as far along as I fear it might be."

The queen shook her head. "As the crown prince, you are allowed broad latitude in any number of things—latitude which your father and I have allowed to go unchecked—but that ends now. There will be no full wing sent to Wisconsin, and the soldiers sent to deal with the incursion will most definitely not be under your command. I'm reassigning you to the Jerusalem Battalion. You'll be leaving in the morning."

Jerek hadn't been making any kind of secret of the fact that he was unhappy with his mother, but her last proclamation seemed to be the final straw for him. Rather than just looking like he was tired of negotiating with her, he actually looked furious.

"Have you listened to anything I've said? We're up against something entirely new, and regardless of whether the incursion so far consists of just three hunters or a thousand hunters, we need to understand how this group is managing to cloak their presence so effectively. If we can't understand how they're doing this, it's entirely possible that we'll be looking at incursions along every dormant portal in both hemispheres, incursions we won't even know are taking place until after they've summoned elders into our world. Please don't let your petty frustrations with me endanger every man, woman and child we, as a race, are responsible for protecting."

The queen suddenly looked tired. She shook her head as though wishing she didn't have to be the one to say what needed to be said.

"I've heard every word you've said, Jerek, but hearing is not the same thing as believing. As much as I would like to believe that your self-imposed isolation hasn't started getting to you, these kind of wild allegations are simply too hard to believe."

"What have I ever done to give you reason to doubt my competence, Mother?"

"You give me reason at every turn to doubt the competence you're so proud of. You dismiss the act of bonding as a barbaric, costly ritual, which you seem to have no willingness to enter into, while forgetting that that ritual is the only way for our race to survive. Not only does it give us much-needed strength on the battlefield, it is vital to our very ability to propagate as a species. What healthy gargoyle could possibly want his entire species to become extinct? Given the fact that your accusations contradict thousands of years of experience of fighting the hunters, how am I to believe them?"

Jerek didn't look any less angry, but there was a hint of something else in his manner now—in someone else it might've looked like fear, but I got the feeling that Jerek wasn't scared, he was just tired of the endless fight that was such an integral component of his interactions with his parents.

"You know that I'm telling the truth. Your gift is telling you that I haven't lied about what happened, and yet still you refuse to believe me."

"My gift has only told me that you believe what you're saying. Based on all of the factors I must consider, I'm forced to assume that the stress of your recent responsibilities has resulted in you seeing terrible new enemies where none exist. My decision to reassign you stands. Say goodbye to your friends. You'll be flying back to Jerusalem with me first thing tomorrow morning."

Chapter 12

After the queen dismissed us from her presence, the three of us were escorted back to our rooms by the same four gargoyles the queen apparently intended on sending out to deal with the hunters back in Wisconsin. Jerek didn't say anything on the way back to our rooms, and Caine and I followed his lead. Once we arrived, Jerek went inside his room and closed the door, leaving Caine and me in the common room with all four of the gargoyles who apparently had been ordered to stand guard on us until the queen left with Jerek.

By that point, I had so many questions I almost didn't know where to start, so I was relieved when Caine took my arm and led me into his room. He dropped the black bag carrying his clothes on the floor and then made a beeline to the closet.

"Well, I'm glad that's over. It didn't go particularly well, but at least it's over and I can get out of this monkey suit. I know that you're probably freaking out right now, but if Jerek went off script like that, then it was for a good reason. He's probably in his room right now figuring out how to turn this apparent setback into a rousing victory."

Freaking out didn't even begin to cover it, and for the first time since my emotions came back I found myself wishing for a little of the emotionless calm I'd experienced after Jerek and I had touched. I wanted to yell and scream, but all I could do was take Caine at his word. I'd accepted the risks when I'd told Jerek that I wanted to go with the alternate plan. Maybe it had been stupid to put that kind of trust in Jerek, but Caine had vouched for him, and it had felt right at the time.

Yelling at Caine wasn't going to fix anything, all I could do was wait for Jerek to explain his backup plan and hope that it would at least work to get us out of Utah. A life on the run was looking better by the moment, but I tried to push all of that to one side and focus on the moment as Caine rummaged through the selection of clothes available to him. After several seconds he finally settled on a pair of jeans and a black T-shirt that was nearly a perfect match for the one Jerek had worn to see his mother.

"I'm not sure that's all that much of an improvement."

"That's because you don't know what I'm about to do to them."

Even as Caine spoke, he started unbuttoning his shirt and I felt my face redden as I realized he fully intended on changing right there in the middle of the room. I quickly turned my back to him and then closed my eyes for good measure.

"What would you've done if I decided to call your bluff?"

"I would've given you the show of your life." I heard Caine slip off his slacks and pull the jeans on, and then a few seconds later the sound of ripping denim brought me back around even though I wasn't completely convinced it was safe to open my eyes. Caine was still shirtless, but at least he'd buttoned up his jeans before he started ripping big holes in them. Once he was satisfied with the number and placement of the tears in his jeans, he started worrying at the edges of the rips, fraying the material so that the rips wouldn't look so artificial.

"If my dad saw you doing that he would freak out. He hates paying money for new jeans that are already halfway worn out, but I think watching someone rip a perfectly good set of pants would send him through the roof."

Caine smiled. "Fortunately, Her Royal Highness, Cyrene Hammerfell, feels much the same way. Despite being richer than the queen of England and all of the billionaires in Monte Carlo combined, she absolutely hates it when I destroy a perfectly good set of clothes. Do you think I'll get another chance to see her before I get sent off to my new assignment?"

I shook my head in bewilderment. "I don't even begin to have enough of an understanding of what's going on here to answer a question like that, Caine, and you know it. Why does Jerek hate his mother so much, and does she really have a power that lets her know when someone is lying to her?"

Caine sighed and then walked over to the bed and sat down, pulling me down next to him. "Are you really sure you want to dive that deep down the rabbit hole, Alice? The white creatures you'll find at the bottom are a lot more dangerous than any fluffy bunny you'll ever come across. I've tried not to get into all the gory details because I thought it was going to make it harder for you to go back to your normal life after Jerek and I were reassigned, but I guess that's a moot point now.

"I have no idea what Jerek has planned, but I rather suspect that it's going to be spectacular, and you might not be the only one living on the run after this."

It suddenly hit me just how selfish I'd been. I'd been focused on what was going to happen to me, and never thought how things were going to change for Caine.

"I'm so sorry, Caine. I didn't think things through enough to realize that there might be consequences for you and Jerek. You have a good thing going in Wisconsin and now I've ruined that too."

"Don't worry about it, Dani. It's not like my social life is really going to get worse than it already is, but if you really feel bad, we can go back to your room and see if the closet has a pair of yoga pants in it. I would gladly trade away my entire future to watch you model something like that for a mere five minutes."

I punched him gently in the shoulder for being such a tease, but I didn't really mean it. My mind was already poking at his words much like his free hand continued to worry at his jeans. I'd never realized it before now, but it was becoming apparent to me that underneath his devil-may-care exterior, Caine was just as lonely as I was.

"What did you mean when you said I might be surprised by the state of your social life?"

Caine winced a little as I asked the question, but he put on a brave smile nonetheless. "Your questions are stacking up faster than I can answer them. Are you really sure that's the thing you want answered next?"

"Don't get me wrong, I still want to know what the heck is going on and what the deal is with Jerek's mom, but I think this question is the one that's most important to you, so it's the one I want answered."

"Fair enough, then answer it I shall. The truth is that I haven't always been friends with Jerek. Even just five or six years ago, he was a royally stuck-up jerk who had no use for any of the rest of us lesser mortals."

I pulled back in shock and gave Caine a skeptical look. "Wait, you mean he used to be worse than he is now? How is that even possible?"

"Be nice, Dani."

"I'm trying to be nice, but Jerek isn't exactly making it easy. Unlike you, he wasn't overjoyed to meet me, and since then he's lied to me, and been alternately hot and cold to the point where I don't even know what to think about him. For all I know, he just threw me to the wolves."

Caine tilted his head to one side and looked at me with an unusually serious expression. "Has he been mean to you?"

I racked my brain trying to remember our earliest interactions and realized that I wasn't actually sure how to answer. "I don't think so, but I couldn't say for sure. If he hasn't been mean to me, then it's only been by the slimmest of margins. I can tell you that he hasn't been particularly nice to me."

"That's the thing about Jerek. Back in the day he was a real prick. That's all changed, but he still uses that same persona as a defense mechanism. If you don't know him very well, it's easy to mistake the persona for the real Jerek."

"I think you're losing me. If Jerek still acts the same way as he did back when you hated his guts, how can you be so sure that he's changed?"

STONE HEART

"Because he's my only friend. I know that probably doesn't make a lot of sense, but there's a lot of background that I'm going to have to explain to you before you'll understand. The long and the short of it is that my parents—before they died—shamed themselves in a way that not very many of my kind do. I grew up not just an orphan, but the orphan of traitors, someone whom nobody wanted to get too close to for fear that whatever had caused my parents to make such terrible decisions would rub off on them like some kind of disease."

I hadn't expected things to get so real so quickly—not with Caine of all people—but my heart went out to him as I started to understand at least some of what he must have gone through growing up.

"I'm so sorry, Caine. I thought I had it rough, but beating guys off with a stick because of some stupid curse is nothing compared to what you went through. How young were you when they died?"

"I was six, and Jerek didn't befriend me until we were twelve, so it was six long years where adults kept me at arm's length and children tormented me every chance they got. Initially Jerek was just as bad as the rest of them. Actually, that's not quite true. Much like what you just described, Jerek was rarely, if ever, directly mean to me, but during those early years he was never nice. That wouldn't have been so bad except for the fact that his being crown prince meant that everyone else took that as tacit permission to see if they could break me."

I reached over and took his left hand in mine, squeezing it in an attempt to show solidarity. The normal Caine would have favored me with some kind of lewd expression and said something to make me blush, but this newer, more vulnerable Caine simply returned the squeeze and then took a deep breath and continued his story.

"All that changed when we turned twelve. Between one day and the next, Jerek went from being passively mean to me to actively defending me to the other kids. I spent a week convinced that I'd fallen and hit my head while out on the playground.

"It seems silly to say it now, but I was unable to come up with any other explanation for why Jerek, of all people, would undergo such a drastic change. Once I finally came to terms with the fact that I wasn't in a coma somewhere hallucinating, I spent two more years waiting for the other shoe to drop. I thought that Jerek was just setting me up for more humiliation down the road, that his father had put him up to it and he was doing all of those nice things under duress, or that he would just wake up one day and realize that he despised me as much as he ever had, but none of that turned out to be the case. Against all odds, our friendship stuck."

I shook my head in amazement, almost unable to believe there had been so much pain in Caine's backstory. "What made it happen? Why did Jerek undergo such a transformation?"

"I wish I knew. When it first happened, everything was too fresh and I was too nervous to poke at it for fear that it would cause him to revert back to his previous ways, but later on I asked him point-blank and he refused to tell me. I think—other than state secrets—that's the only thing that Jerek's ever refused to explain to me.

"All I can remember is that he had just come back from a trip to Utah to spend time with his mother when everything changed. It wasn't just his treatment of me either. Before that, Jerek lived a life of privilege the likes of which even after seeing this place you still probably can't really envision. He was the perfect heir to the throne, and the apple of his parents' eyes, but something big must've happened while he was here in Utah with them. When he got back it seemed like the three of them couldn't see eye to eye on anything.

"The royal line has served in the heavy strike section of the guard for as long as there's been a guard. Jerek had been training for that since shortly after he learned how to walk, but after that trip he tried to change his military training track. He tried to become a scout like me—and would have at that, if his parents hadn't thrown the world's biggest fit."

I shifted on the bed, wishing that there was a way for Caine to just dump all of this information in my mind. I was giving it my best, but his answers continued to raise more questions than I could keep track of. Luckily Caine seemed to pick up on my frustration.

"The guard is made up of essentially three groups. The scouts are responsible for keeping track of dormant portals and tracking down stray hunters who slip through our lines in an attempt to set up new incursion fronts. We're the least prestigious group, which is ironic given that in a lot of ways what we do is the most dangerous.

"Unlike the other two branches of the guard, I can't run around all hours of the day carrying a massive two-handed sword, which means when I do run into a hunter, I have to fight it with my bare hands and hope for the best. Things don't always turn out the way you might hope. The hunters might look like stupid freaky animals, but even the stupidest of them has a kind of animal cunning that makes them incredibly dangerous. They are more than capable of working together in a cooperative fashion, and they've gotten really creative at coming up with ways to ambush us despite the fact that we can usually smell them coming."

"That actually makes a lot of sense. It seemed like it was all Jerek could do to fight off the one hunter back on the island, but you managed to survive for at least a couple of minutes against two hunters all by yourself."

"Yeah, that's because of the difference in our training. I've been learning how to fight with my hands for as long as I can remember, while Jerek has spent all of that time learning how to use a variety of heavy weapons. All things considered, he's still pretty good with his hands, but he's at least an order of magnitude more dangerous when you give him a weapon. If he'd been armed when that hunter attacked you guys, it would've taken Jerek less than five seconds to dispatch it, while if you gave me a weapon I probably would've just chopped off my own foot."

"So the scouts…scout…everything, and the heavy strike branch runs around with the kind of massive weapons I saw in Jerek's bedroom. What does the third branch of the guard do?"

"We don't just 'scout', we're also responsible for damage control among the humans. Typically we are the best at compulsion, which is why we're assigned where we're assigned."

I held up my free hand. "I'm sorry, I didn't mean to minimize your role in the conflict."

"That's right, I get enough of that from everyone else and I don't need it from you too." The words could have come across as harsh, but for the first time since we'd started talking about all of this, Caine once again had a smile on his face. He was mostly just giving me a hard time.

"The heavy strike guys and gals are the ones who get sent into the worst of the fighting. Think of them as shock troops from hell and you'll pretty much have the right idea. The third branch consists of people who wanted to make it into the heavy strike troops, but who lacked the size and strength, or who just weren't deadly enough to go up against the biggest and baddest the hunters have to offer. They call themselves the Cavalry, but the rest of us just call them squires. They're responsible for bottling up incursions and supporting the flanks of any heavy strike units that are deployed in the area. Individually, they're nowhere near as dangerous as the heavy strike, but there's a lot more of them, so an awful lot of the fighting still ends up falling on them."

I shrugged. "It sounds to me like you got the best end out of that deal, my friend. While the heavy strike and the squires are busy fighting and dying, you get to hang out with beautiful women like *moi*. I mean, it sounds like people bust your chops and stuff, but from the standpoint of actual lifestyle, it pretty much seems like yours is the way to go."

Caine nodded distractedly, but he'd released my hand and was back to picking at the fraying spots on his jeans. I realized for the first time that he was beyond just nervous. He was worried that I was going to respond poorly to the rest of what he had to say.

"There are other factors, Dani, but before I tell you what they are, I need you to promise me that you'll hear me out."

"Okay, I promise."

He shook his head at me, a trace of frustration starting to leak past his worry. "I'm serious, Dani. I need you to really promise. You need to assume I'm going to tell you the worst thing imaginable, and still promise me that you're willing to hear me out before you go running out of this room."

With somebody else, being told something like that would've scared me, but with Caine I just couldn't believe it was going to be as bad as he was indicating. I did a quick mental survey to check if he was trying to compel me, but there was no sense of pressure in my mind. It was nothing more sinister than the fact that I liked and trusted him.

"I have a hard time believing that you've done anything close to the worst thing I can imagine, Caine, but I promise that I will hear you out regardless of how bad things turn out to be. Is that good enough?"

"I don't know, but it's the best I can realistically expect, so I guess here goes nothing." I waited for a moment as Caine worked up his courage. "Did you catch the bit during the argument between Jerek and his mom where she mentioned bonding, and the fact that the survival of our race depends on it?"

"Yeah, that was on my list of questions—we just hadn't made it that far yet."

Caine took a deep breath. "We gargoyles are sterile in our natural state, Dani."

I gave him a confused look. "You just finished telling me that you had parents, Caine. Doesn't that kind of, by definition, indicate that you're not all sterile?"

"Yeah, that's where the bonding comes in. In our natural state, we're sterile, but we don't have to remain that way. There is a very small percentage of the human population—less than a fraction of one percent—who have the ability to bond with gargoyles, and reverse our natural state."

On the face of it, what he was describing seemed fairly benign, but Caine wasn't wearing the expression of someone who'd just shared a harmless piece of information—which meant there had to be a lot more to the process of bonding someone than I was assuming.

"So, what's involved in being bonded?"

"You could think of it as a mystical wedding ceremony, but it's a lot more than that."

"Just go ahead and spit it out, Caine. The suspense is killing me and I can almost guarantee that the reality isn't as bad as what I'm envisioning."

Caine didn't look like he was convinced, but he nodded and proceeded with this explanation. "Finding a human who has the potential to be bonded is a difficult process in and of itself. In theory, any gargoyle could bond with any eligible human, but some humans are more attuned to bond with certain gargoyles than others. The only sure way for one of us to know that we've found a human who can be bonded is to touch them."

"That's why you were so handsy when I first met you, wasn't it? You were trying to find out whether I was someone you could bond with."

Caine nodded. "Yeah, there aren't a ton of chances to meet new people in a town as small as Clay, so when I saw you for the first time I hurried over to see if you had the potential to be bonded."

"I take it that I don't—at least not with you?"

"Sometimes touching someone results in an inconclusive kind of reading, which really just means that the gargoyle in question can't bond them, but that it's possible someone else could. Other times we get a definite sense that the individual in question can't be bonded. You are one of the latter, Dani. Sending energy into you was like sending it into a black hole."

I felt a surge of disappointment at the news, which was ridiculous given that I still didn't know what being bonded entailed, but the feeling was undeniable.

"Okay, so I'm not bonding material. What does that mean?"

"Well, not to put too fine a point on it, when you combine it with the fact that you're immune to compulsion, it means that you never have to worry about any of my kind forcing you to do anything you don't want to do."

"That sounds awfully ominous."

"You might not want to be so quick to dismiss it, Dani. Bonding happens in two stages. The first step is fairly innocuous. It involves nothing more than skin-to-skin contact between the gargoyle and the human in question, with an intent on the side of the gargoyle to establish a preliminary bond with the human."

Caine was starting to make me really nervous, but I was committed to hearing him out now. I took a deep breath and nodded for him to go on.

"The first stage of the bonding serves no immediate purpose other than to make it so that no one else can bond with that particular human. It does, however, set into motion a chain of events that can't be reversed. Neither the human nor the gargoyle reaps any kind of benefits from the first stage of the bond, but the gargoyle immediately becomes more attracted to the human in question. It starts out as something very easy to dismiss, but as the days and weeks go by it continues to grow in intensity until the second stage of the bond is completed."

"So what happens when the second stage is completed?"

"It depends on how much time passed between the first stage and the second stage, but invariably the side effects of completing the bonding for my people include—among other things—increased strength, speed, the ability to manifest wings on a long-term basis, and improved resistance to the hunters' claws. Basically, being bonded turns even a lowly scout like me into someone who could go toe-to-toe with two or even three heavy strike fighters at the same time. It elevates even the least of us into being the best of us."

I shrugged. "Which means that once you bond you're even better able to fight off the hunters, right? When you add in the fact that it makes it so you can have a bunch of little Caines running around, it seems like a pretty good deal to me. I'm not sure what you're freaking out about."

"The emotions that the gargoyle side of the bond feels during the time between when the bond is started and when it's completed don't just evaporate, Dani. They're still present, and if the bond has been growing for long enough they can be overpowering. Usually the attraction and dedication are moved from the gargoyle to the human half of the bond, and if a long time has passed since the first part of the bond occurred, it can lead to the human losing their ability to make their own choices."

I was well and truly freaked out by that point, but in too much shock to get up and run out of the room like I would have otherwise. "Wait, so you're saying that the humans all get turned into some kind of weird love slaves for the gargoyles?"

Caine shook his head. "Not always. If the bond is completed right away, then the humans still have the ability to make their own decisions. They'll have strong feelings of affection towards their gargoyle, but potentially it's nothing more than what you or I feel towards each other."

"Go ahead and let the other shoe drop, Caine. I can tell that you're holding something back. If that's the way things work, why would anyone ever choose to stretch out the initial bond more than just a few seconds?"

"Because the size of the advantages we gargoyles receive from the bond grow in direct relation to how long the bond is left at the preliminary stages. A bond that only settles for a day or two will allow the gargoyle to fly and will make them stronger and faster, but they'll still barely stand out from the other members of the heavy strike branch. A bond which is allowed to mature for weeks, or even months, has the capability of bestowing abilities that allow a single gargoyle to successfully stand up to even one of the hunter elders."

"So you guys purposely take away people's freedom of choice? You run around touching everyone you can get your hands on, and then once you find a likely candidate, you establish the first stage of the bond and then compel them to stay by your side until you get to the point where the bond can make you truly powerful? I think I'm going to be sick."

I wasn't joking, I could feel my last meal—something we'd picked up at a fast-food joint just outside of Salt Lake—starting to come up, but Caine grabbed my arm as I stood and refused to let go.

"It's not like that, Dani. I wasn't going to do that. Yes, I wanted to bond somebody, but I wasn't going to drag things out. I was going to bond them just long enough to get myself some wings and then I was going to complete the bond while they still had the ability to choose for themselves what they were going to do with their lives."

"I don't care what justifications you've created for yourself, Caine, what you are planning on doing is wrong. Compelling someone to be some kind of gargoyle baby machine is uncon-scionable."

Caine winced, which could've simply been a response to my indictment of his lifestyle, but I could tell that there was something else beneath the surface. He still hadn't let go of me, so I stood there looking at him expectantly waiting to see if he would finish coming clean or if he would take the coward's way out.

"It's not like that, Dani. I wasn't going to compel anybody. I would only enter into a bond with someone who understood what they were getting into. It would be her choice, and if she said no then I would walk away and never bother her again. Not only that, I would make sure she was well compensated for what she was giving up. Regardless of whether or not she wanted to stay with me, I would make sure she was taken care of for the rest of her life."

"What do you mean you would make sure she was well compensated for what she was giving up? You were planning on buying her babies off of her?"

"No, it's not like that at all, Dani. The bond makes us fertile after it's finalized, but it doesn't make it so we can have babies with humans. It just makes it so that we can have babies with other gargoyles."

"So what would she be giving up?"

Caine refused to look at me as he answered. "The second stage of the bond makes the human side of the bond sterile. Whoever I bond would never be able to have babies of their own."

Chapter 13

I felt like I'd been slapped. The concept of an entire race of people who survived by serving as parasites to people like me was something I was having a hard time coming to grips with, but before I could come up with a response Jerek threw the door open and walked into Caine's room.

"Good, you're ready to go, Caine. Here, Dani, put these on so that you're ready when it's time to move."

As he spoke, Jerek tossed some jeans and a T-shirt onto the bed where I'd been sitting just a few moments earlier. His other hand was holding sneakers that looked like they were the same size as the dress shoes I'd put on before going to the audience with his mother.

"If you think I'm going anywhere with either of you, then you're stark raving mad."

Jerek looked over at Caine for an explanation, which took surprisingly few words. "I just told her about the bond."

Jerek suddenly looked tired in a way that even having his mother tell him he was being reassigned and forced to leave behind his best friend hadn't been able to manage.

"I'm sorry, Dani. I know how repugnant you must find all of that. Believe it or not, I share your views, but this unfortunately is not the time for any of that."

"No, I'm not going to let you sweet-talk me into thinking that this is all okay. Nobody with a soul could possibly agree to any of this. I'm not leaving this room."

Jerek dropped the sneakers a few inches away from my feet and then looked back up at me with determination in his eyes. "I wish that we lived in a world where that could be the case, but the truth of the matter is that you will be leaving this room sooner or later. If you're really determined not to go with us, I will respect your wishes, but you should know that my mother will not show the same level of consideration. You can't be compelled, which means that you're a security risk of the kind that she would never dream of letting walk out of this house.

"You have a choice, but not the choice you think you have. You can either walk out of here with Caine and me as a free woman—at least for a little while—or you can stay here and allow my mother to imprison you somewhere until she comes up with a way to guarantee that you'll never leak our secret to anyone. I don't honestly expect that she'll put much effort into figuring out a solution to the problem you represent. It wouldn't surprise me if she simply left you locked up until you died of natural causes or she figured out what makes you immune to compulsion."

I'd never been in that kind of position, and it was even more terrifying than I would've guessed. My first instinct was to throw some kind of fit in the hopes that Jerek—and even his mother—would back down to avoid causing a scene, but that was just because I was a product of a civilized society. I'd grown up in a world where things like naked force had long ago become a rare occurrence and somewhere along the way my ancestors and I had lost the ability to function when confronted with it.

I wanted to believe that Jerek was lying to me, that his mother wouldn't actually do something like that, but everything that had happened since I'd left Wisconsin told me he was telling the truth. We locked gazes for several seconds and then I finally reached down and picked up both the shoes and the clothes he'd brought me from my room. I walked over to my bathroom without looking back, and somehow I even managed not to burst into tears.

It took me only a minute or so to slip out of the dress clothes I'd been wearing and into the jeans and T-shirt Jerek had picked out for me. I came back out to find Caine asking questions of Jerek, who seemed unusually reticent.

"You can't really think that there's any way we're going to get out of here. I'm good with my hands, and you're better than the average heavy strike soldier, but even if those were four normal gargoyles out there we still wouldn't be able to take them all by ourselves. When you add in the fact that all four of those are riven, we have no choice. They may not have their bonded humans to draw strength from anymore, but you and I both know that they're still stronger and faster than either of us."

"I don't need you to tell me all of that, Caine. I just need you to be ready to move when the opportunity for escape presents itself. Speaking of which, you really ought to put some shoes on."

Caine grumbled as he headed back in the closet to look for footwear suitable for being on the run from the queen of the gargoyle nation, but he didn't question Jerek after that. I looked back and forth between the two of them with a dizzying mixture of emotions coursing through me. Now that I'd had a second to cool down, I found myself analyzing Jerek's statement. He'd implied that he found the bonding process just as abhorrent as I had, which was promising, but I wasn't sure now was the time to try to get into the philosophical question of whether or not he was really as ready to consign his species to extinction as I was.

Caine came out of the closet and made as if to pull me down onto the bed beside him, but I was in no mood for being teased out of my anger, so I stepped further away and shot him a glare. Things seemed like they were headed towards something worse than just tense when someone knocked on the door to Caine's bedroom.

The man who entered a moment later in response to Jerek's invitation, looked like he was in his forties—basically the same age as Jerek's mom—but that was where the resemblance ended. Where she'd been blonde and imperious, he was dark-haired and looked like someone who should be spoiling his first grandchild or two rather than helping out inside the headquarters of a species of creatures that weren't supposed to exist.

"Did my mother send you to check up on me, Thomas?"

"Not in so many words, but yes. I think she's hoping that I will be able to serve as a bridge between the two of you, much like I used to do when you were but a child, Jerek."

Jerek shook his head. "I think we're long past that point."

Thomas bestowed a gentle smile on me and gave Caine a respectful nod before turning his full attention back to Jerek. "I suspect that you're right, but the truth is that I'm not just here on behalf of your mother. I have missed you these long months, and I was worried if I told her the futility of what she'd asked that she might change my orders and deprive me of the chance to see you."

Thomas looked so forlorn that not even Jerek could remain unaffected by the older man's obvious sorrow. He relented and shook Thomas' hand. That in and of itself would've been out of character for Jerek, but even more surprising was the fact that he allowed himself to be pulled into a hug almost even before the handshake had a chance to get started.

"No matter what happened between now and when we left Salt Lake, you would've still had a chance to see me on the plane that will be taking us over to Jerusalem, Thomas."

The confusion that flashed across Thomas' face was almost as heartbreaking as his loneliness from a moment earlier. "I suppose you're right. I'm afraid this old brain doesn't work like it used to."

"Your problem has nothing to do with old age, my friend, and everything to do with the fact that you're bonded to my mother. What she did to you was a crime. Rather than opting for a light link that would've allowed you to remain essentially the same man you were when she met you, or waiting a few extra months to ensure that there wouldn't be enough of you left to miss what you'd lost, she opted to do neither and scooped out the bulk of your free will while still leaving you enough to realize what you'd lost."

"You know how much it pains me to hear you talk ill of your mother, Jerek. Much has changed since you were first placed into my care, but the simple passage of time would never be enough to erase that particular constant."

Jerek looked as though he was going to respond with something else—probably even more biting—but Thomas turned towards me with another smile. "We're being terribly rude, Jerek. I taught you better than to allow several minutes to pass without introducing lovely young ladies even to decrepit old artifacts like me."

"You're right, I have been remiss. Dani, this is Thomas, the man bonded to my mother, who was responsible for raising me while my parents were off fighting. Thomas, this is Dani Destone, a young woman of unique talents who has been pulled into our world through no fault of her own."

I half expected Thomas to shake my hand like he'd done with Jerek, but he merely bowed respectfully. "Don't let Jerek sour you on his mother. While it's true that being bonded is not without sacrifices, I clearly remember the joy I felt as I agreed to be bonded to my Cyrene."

"I'm sorry if this is disrespectful, but isn't it possible that she compelled you to feel that way?"

Thomas shook his head gently. "No, it's not. The second stage of the bond eliminates all compulsion from before the bonding, and once bonded, we humans are just as immune to compulsion as the gargoyles are. My feelings for her at that moment were completely un-manufactured."

Thomas turned back towards Jerek with an inquiring look. "Can I get the three of you something to eat? Your mother has forbidden anyone from letting you out of the suite, but it would break my heart to know that you were stuck in here until morning without anything to eat."

"No, that won't be necessary, Thomas."

"Are you sure? Morning is a long way off, and you need to keep your strength up if you're headed to the front lines. Let me bring something for your friends and I'll include a little extra. You'll never have to admit to me that you ate some of it once this old man has gone."

Jerek shook his head once again, but as he did so he was overcome by an inexplicable surge of emotion. Up until that point, I hadn't been entirely sure that Jerek was able to feel anything other than boredom, anger, or frustration, but in that moment I saw a sorrow so deep it made my heart ache for him.

Thomas saw the same heartbreaking change in expression and reached out in a vain attempt to comfort the man who'd once been his responsibility, but Jerek gently pushed Thomas' hands away. "I'm sorry for all of this, Thomas."

Before Thomas or any of the rest of us could even begin to wonder what exactly Jerek was apologizing for, he grabbed Thomas and spun him around so that the older man was facing the wall with Jerek's arm around his neck.

"Jerek, what are you doing?"

"Only what I must. If my mother will not see reason, then I will force her to treat this situation with the seriousness it deserves. Caine, get the phone out of his pocket and then dial my mother. Once you've got her on the line, make sure that Dani is sandwiched between you and me. We're going to have to be careful if you want to make sure that nobody gets a chance to take a shot at her."

Caine was just as obviously floored by Jerek's sudden decision to take Thomas hostage, but he responded with the prompt obedience of someone who'd been taking orders his entire life. He pulled me forward so that I was between the two of them, and then dialed Jerek's mother and held the phone up to Jerek's ear.

Say whatever else one might about Jerek's mother, she answered Thomas' call on the second ring.

I was close enough that I was able to hear both sides of the conversation. I wasn't sure if that was a blessing or a curse, but I wasn't about to pass up the chance to listen in.

"This isn't Thomas, Mother, this is Jerek. Unless you want to become one of the riven, you'll instruct your people to provide us with safe passage down to the garage."

There was a pause as the queen tried to wrap her mind around the threat her son had just leveled. "You would never dare kill Thomas. I would have you executed as a traitor so quickly your father wouldn't even have a chance to make it back here in time to see the show."

"I think, under the circumstances, that we can dispense with all the usual posturing, Mother. I'm fully aware that you're able to sense the truth of my words even when communicating by phone at this distance. If you fail to do as I say, I will execute Thomas and leave you nothing but a shadow of your current self. If, on the other hand, you do exactly as I say, I will make sure that Thomas makes it back to you safely. You have my word on it."

"You're right, we can dispense with all of the usual back and forth. Simply by threatening Thomas, you've proved yourself a traitor. If you release him now I'll see to it that you're stripped of your titles and exiled to some unimportant backwater with nothing more than the shirt on your back, but I will spare your life out of consideration for the fact that you are my own flesh and blood. That offer, however, expires the moment you set foot out of this house."

Thomas' hands had been slowly inching back towards me while Jerek had been talking to the queen. I thought nothing of it until Jerek picked Thomas up and all but shook him.

"Don't even think about it, Thomas. Caine and I are fireproof, and if you try to use your powers on Dani I will break your neck before you can do anything more than singe her clothing."

For a second I thought Thomas was still going to try whatever it was that Jerek was warning him against, but then he relaxed his hands back down to a neutral spot at his sides.

"I believe he truly means it, Mistress. As much as I wish it weren't the case, your son seems very much willing to end my life if you refuse to meet his demands. Do you wish me to attempt to harm the girl in spite of that?"

"No, you're more valuable to me than the three of them put together. Jerek is telling the truth that he will release you once he's gotten everything he wants. I'll see to the arrangements."

As quickly as that she hung up and the four of us were left to stand there in silence. Only a minute or two later I heard the four gargoyles who'd been standing guard inside the suite leave, and Jerek started us into motion only seconds after that.

Despite the fact that I was still angry at Caine for hiding such a terrible secret from me, I found myself grateful to have him at my back as we walked through the long, empty corridors between our rooms and the garage. Apparently he and Jerek were confident that their innate resistances to physical damage would allow them to withstand shots from a high-powered rifle, but I had no such ability and given the coldness in the queen's tone as she'd talked about executing her son, I was pretty sure that she wouldn't hesitate to order her people to kill me if they had the chance.

I'd been expecting us to go directly down to the vehicles, but instead Jerek led us to an unfamiliar-looking hallway only a few dozen yards from where we'd started out. Before I could ask what was going on, Jerek ordered Thomas to run his thumb across the biometric lock so that we could get inside. Once we were inside, I was greeted with an array of weapons that showed up even what I'd seen in Jerek's bedroom.

"Grab me a hammer, and arm yourself with whatever you want, Caine. If I'm right about what's waiting for us in Wisconsin, we're not going to want to walk into it unarmed."

Jerek continued to maintain his hold on Thomas as Caine quickly searched through the racks of weapons before picking up a massive two-handed hammer and a pair of long daggers.

"What if you're wrong about how far along the infestation is?"

"Then you're going to get shuffled off to somewhere even more unpleasant than what my mom already had in mind for you, but if we're both honest she was already planning on sticking you in the worst hole she could find. This just means she's going to try a little harder."

"Yeah, I figured that was about the shape of things, but what about you?"

"If I'm wrong, then Mother is going to try to execute me just like she said she would, but I'm not just going to roll over and die. Too much depends on me to let her get away with that."

Caine nodded. "Good. I just wanted to make sure we're on the same page there. I'm not going to stand by and let her chop your head off either."

The rest of the trip down to the garage wasn't exactly uneventful, but we made it without anybody dying, and given our circumstances, I was feeling like that was a pretty big achievement. We passed several dozen guards located at the far end of various corridors, but after the first time it happened Jerek ordered Thomas to call the queen again and let her know that any guards we ran into had better not be carrying weapons if she wanted to get her pet human back in one piece.

Jerek had demanded that the garage be emptied out before we made it down there, and it was, but I was pretty sure that wasn't fooling any of us. He'd been hoping to make it harder for his mother's people to follow us, but the truth was that she probably already had half a dozen cars stationed at strategic points around the estate. There was no way for us to guarantee that someone wasn't going to attack us the moment our guard was lowered.

Caine did a quick inspection of a big black SUV in one corner of the garage, and then once he pronounced it free of bombs, or any obvious electronic surveillance, all four of us climbed in. Caine took the spot directly behind the driver's seat, which was where Thomas was told to sit, while I sat next to Caine and Jerek took up a position next to our hostage.

Once we were on the road and Jerek was satisfied that whatever units his mother had tailing us were staying far enough back they weren't immediately obvious, Thomas was ordered to call the Queen back and tell her we wanted a plane prepped. It probably shouldn't have surprised me that Jerek's family had access to a private jet, but the fact that Thomas specified one particular jet was an indication that they had more than one plane just in Salt Lake.

"We'll need to give the pilot a destination so they can make sure there is sufficient fuel to arrive safely, and so they can file an appropriate flight plan."

Jerek shook his head. "The destination is Clay, Wisconsin, just like I said it would be, but we're not bringing along another pilot. You're going to fly the plane, Thomas. After all, it's about time you got some use out of that pilot's license my mother ordered you to get."

Thomas pulled his eyes off of the road for just long enough to give Jerek an apologetic look. "I am sorry about that. I never meant to go back on my promise to you, but your mother said it was important and I always figured we could put your telescope together at another time."

"Yeah, I know you're sorry, but the funny thing about once-in-a-lifetime celestial events is that there isn't another time. Don't worry about it, I'm past it. Besides, we both know it's not your fault. The bond means that you don't have the ability to make your own choices when it comes to things like that."

The four of us passed the rest of the drive out to the airport in uncomfortable silence, but I was pretty sure it was preferable to the alternative. I kept expecting something to go wrong. Normal airport security never would've permitted the four of us onto a plane carrying knives and a massive battle hammer that was nearly as tall as I was, but apparently things were different when you were flying out on a private plane. We didn't even go to the main airport. Instead we pulled up to a smaller, secondary airfield that was adjacent to the main airport, and no one even looked at us twice as we walked through the lobby and out to the hangar where the plane was being prepped for takeoff.

I wasn't sure whether that was because Caine and Jerek were hard at work compelling everyone not to look very closely at us, or if security at private airports was just really that lax, but I was grateful that it was one less thing to worry about. The next fifteen minutes seemed to drag out forever, but all things considered, it was remarkable that we were able to get queued up to taxi so quickly.

Jerek disappeared into the cockpit with Thomas, which just left Caine and me sitting in the lavishly upholstered main cabin. I had no desire to pick up our conversation where we'd left it, and pulled out my phone so that I could pretend to be enthralled by something on the screen, but Caine apparently was unwilling to forgo a chance to pick at the fraying threads of what remained of our friendship.

"You have every reason to be mad at me, but I just want you to know that not all of us are like Jerek's mom. The worst of us are exactly like you think, finding some poor, innocent human and bonding them in such a way as to guarantee maximum power on our side of things, and maximum pliability on theirs, but there's a whole range of behavior that I think you would find less objectionable from there.

"Jerek, for instance, passed up multiple opportunities to bond with girls found by other gargoyles who were already bonded. The fact that he's the crown prince means he gets first pick of any humans who are found by a bonded member of our kind, but he's absolutely unwilling to bond on those kinds of terms."

I put my phone away with a heavy sigh and turned to give Caine my full attention. "Great. Bully for him, but the way you said that means there are circumstances under which he's more than willing to take away the free will and fertility of some poor girl. You'll have to excuse me if I'm underwhelmed by his awesomeness."

"You still don't understand. Jerek isn't just some guy, he's the heir to the throne of a kingdom that's been at war since before people started recording history on cave walls. If he told his mother he was unwilling to ever bond someone it would be a complete breach of protocol. She would have passed him over for his brother years ago."

"So she passes him over, big deal. There are some people who would say that not violating someone's ability to choose her future is more important than becoming the next king."

"Right, because Jerek's mother is totally the kind of individual who is willing to entertain threats to the succession. You've met her now, and I'm pretty sure you picked up the same vibe that I've been getting from her for the last six or seven years. If Jerek really convinced her that it was in her best interest to let him abdicate his claim to the throne, it would only be a matter of time before she decided that the best way to guarantee his brother's succession was to make sure that Jerek wouldn't be around to reconsider his decision to step down. For Jerek, this isn't just a matter of inheriting a throne, this is a matter of life and death."

I opened my mouth to tell Caine that I didn't care what happened to Jerek, but he kept talking without giving me a chance to get a word in edgewise. "Jerek is a romantic. He said he'll bond, but only if he falls in love with someone and then later on finds out that there's a possibility they could bond. He's effectively saying that bonding and continuing the royal line isn't as important to him as finding someone he can truly see himself with on a long-term basis. That kind of declaration almost never happens anymore, but tradition grants him the right to do that as long as he's actively looking for a mate."

"So it's all just a ploy? Jerek needed a way to get his mom off his back, so he picks the least likely method of finding someone to bond that he could think of? That doesn't seem particularly heroic."

"No, Dani, there's still too much you don't understand. If the circumstances were different then maybe that could be what was going on, but Jerek's mom isn't just a regular gargoyle."

"Yeah, I got that. She's the queen."

"Yeah, but it's more than just that. All gargoyles are stronger and faster than your average human, but some gargoyles have a little extra edge. They manifest what we call talents. Jerek's mom has the ability to tell whether or not someone is lying to her."

He caught me so off guard that I did a double-take as his words finally registered. There had been so many hints along the way, but I'd never managed to put two and two together. "You're saying she's like a human—I mean gargoyle—lie detector?"

"Yeah, and there's no way that she would buy off on Jerek lying about something like that, so he's telling the truth."

I shook my head in astonishment. What Caine was telling me matched up with the conversation between Jerek and his mother, but it still seemed too incredible to be real. I'd had the existence of the gargoyles and the hunters shoved into my face in such a way that I hadn't been able to dispute them, but that was nothing compared to the idea that some of them had abilities like what Caine had just described.

"How many of you can do stuff like that? Is it common?"

"No, in fact, that's a big part of why Jerek's family has remained on the throne for so many centuries. His lineage has manifested more talents than any other group of gargoyles in history. His father is a seer, and there have been a number of times his talent has saved large groups of gargoyles from being cut off and destroyed by the hunters."

"What about Jerek? Does he have a talent?"

"Yeah, but it's been a big disappointment to his parents. Jerek is able to see who someone is and what they have the potential to become. To be honest, that's probably part of why he underwent such a stark change a few years back. His talent had already started to manifest before then, but nothing like it is now. I suspect he got really tired of having people pretend to be one way to his face while knowing the entire time that they weren't actually the person they were trying to portray themselves as."

I suddenly felt a strong connection to Jerek. For so many years now I'd grappled with thinking a guy was one way only to find out days or weeks later that he was a completely different person than what he presented to the outside world. Time and time again, I'd hoped that some guy who was under the influence of my curse would be one of the nice ones who turned and ran as soon as they figured out I wasn't going to date them, but all too often I'd watched in horror as one of them started exhibiting the behavior of someone who was all too likely to end up assaulting some poor girl over the next few years.

I'd long felt that having a special insight into the character of those around me was more of a burden than a gift, and knowing that Jerek was suffering under a similar cross gave me a different perspective on him. Somehow, that one fact outweighed everything else I knew about him. The fact that he was rich and the heir to a throne just didn't seem to matter when stacked up against him being forced to know just how fake most people really were.

I nearly let the conversation end right there, but there was one other thing that was still tickling the back of my mind. "You said that your parents were considered traitors. Why was that, Caine?"

Caine had already been looking uncomfortable, but what I saw on his face now took things to a whole other level. "I was hoping you wouldn't ask me about that."

"It's not like I'm going to judge you any more harshly than I already have. Why don't you just go ahead and tell me?"

"Because I don't want you to feel like I'm trying to manipulate you." Caine looked at me expectantly but I motioned for him to go on.

He waited, as though giving me an opportunity to change my mind, and then sighed. "There's one other thing I haven't told you about the bonding process, Dani. The strength of the bond does indeed depend on how much time passes between the first part and the second part of the bond, but it doesn't always have to end with the humans as the slaves. If the gargoyles in question are selfless enough, they can keep the obsession from targeting the human half of the bond, and take it upon themselves."

"Wait, so you're saying that the gargoyles end up being slaves to the humans?"

"Yes, nearly everything else about the bond remains the same. The gargoyles become fertile and the humans become sterile, but instead of the gargoyles becoming part of the governing elite, they're relegated to the rank of outcasts. Things aren't quite as bad if the humans they bonded join the military, but they're still looked down on because humans don't make very good war-riors—at least not in comparison to gargoyles."

"Why is that?"

"Humans who are bonded become stronger, but not as strong as a gargoyle who's bonded. The same thing goes for their resistance to physical damage, but the real kicker is that humans were never meant to fly. The human who is the dominant partner in a bond gains wings just like the gargoyle would have, but your minds just aren't as adapted to three-dimensional thinking as ours are. It's considered to be the ultimate waste in a bond.

"Now that we understand the way the genetics work, there's a constant worry that by bonding humans we're taking whatever trait allows them to be bonded out of the gene pool and reducing its prevalence in the general population, so not only do we lose a gargoyle who could otherwise help turn the tide in a key battle, those humans are no longer able to produce offspring that could be bonded at a future date."

"So that's what happened with your parents, isn't it? They bonded but they chose not to be the dominant partner in the relationship."

"Yeah. They knew each other—there are few enough gargoyles who've completed a stage one bonding that they pretty much would've had to have known each other—but they didn't actually go into things knowing that the other person was planning on doing the same thing they were. There was just too much of a stigma for anybody to admit something like that.

"My dad was the one who completed his bonding first, which I'm told is part of what gave my mother the courage required to go through with her plans as well. She left a note for the man she bonded asking him to pair her with my father. She didn't know him well, but it's common practice to try to keep subordinate gargoyles pregnant as much as possible."

Caine cleared his throat, obviously fighting strong emotion, but still trying to finish his story. "The humans my parents bonded were good people. They didn't love each other, but they did what they could to help in the fight against the hunters, and they tried to make sure that I was well taken care of."

"How did your parents die? If it's too painful to talk about I understand, but I would really like to know."

"No, it's okay, I can talk about it. The bond lasts for as long as both parties are alive, but there's a noticeable decrease in its effectiveness when the human and the gargoyle in question are separated by large amounts of distance. Because of that, I was moved around a lot growing up, which is common for gargoyle children. The humans kept my parents close so that they would have every advantage possible when they went into a fight, but because my parents and I were so looked down upon inside of gargoyle society, I wasn't with the rest of the gargoyle kids in the area.

"Gargoyle nurseries are some of the most strongly defended locations on the planet, but out of deference to the way my parents were treated, the humans had established a secondary location for us to stay at while they were out fighting."

"The hunters got to you, didn't they?"

"Yeah, they did. It wasn't a massive strike force, but it was big enough to do the job. The bond meant that my parents weren't always very with it—kind of the way that Thomas seems to have a hard time tracking all the way to the end of a chain of thoughts sometimes—but they managed to hide me inside the closet and then gave their lives in an attempt to fight off the hunters. They were both killed, but they got word out in time to get a heavy strike force headed our direction, and reinforcements arrived before the hunters could finish ransacking our home."

"You said yesterday that you'd been on your own for a long time. The humans they bonded weren't willing to take over raising you after that?"

Caine shook his head. "They probably would have, but humans don't survive the death of the gargoyle half of the bond. Whatever it is that gives them the extended life expectancy as a result of the bond seems to come from us, and once we die, they die too."

I probably should've been angry. It was yet another thing that the humans who were bonded gave up—sometimes without even being given the choice beforehand—but I just couldn't seem to get past the overwhelming sense of sympathy I had for what Caine had been through. The emotion was too much, too soon after everything else I'd been through over the last couple days, and I found myself looking for distraction by asking about things that didn't really matter.

"So when the gargoyles die the humans die too, but it's not the same the other way around, is it?"

"No, it's not. When the human half of the link dies the gargoyle survives and becomes one of the riven. They're still stronger and faster than normal gargoyles, and they keep the power of flight, but they are only a shadow of their former selves and they lose the ability to control fire."

Jerek's concern about where Thomas' hands had been pointing suddenly made a lot of sense. "So you guys can shoot fire out of your fingertips too?"

"Yeah, sorry. I kind of forgot about that."

I reached over and gave Caine's hand a squeeze. "I'm really sorry about what happened to your parents and how you were treated growing up. Were you planning on doing the same thing your parents did if you found some-one to bond?"

Caine shrugged, still looking miserable. "I wish I could give you an honest answer one way or another, Dani. I've spent my entire life pretending I didn't care about other people's approval, but the truth is that I crave it. I know that turning someone into a slave is the kind of thing no decent person should contemplate, but by the same stretch of imagination the last thing I want is for some kid of mine to go through what I went through growing up.

"I told myself time and time again that it would be okay if I bonded someone and just kept the bonding light enough that they still had all of their agency, but I have to admit there are times that I worry I won't be able to resist the temptation to delay finalizing the bond by just a few more days in an effort to buy myself just that much more respect once I finally complete the bond. The idea of that kind of power is a lot more seductive than I realized it would be when I was a kid fantasizing about being ushered into the nobility."

I still didn't approve of the way it sounded like some of the gargoyles chose to pursue their bonds, but now that I'd heard the rest of Caine's story I was starting to feel a lot less judgmental about those gargoyles who legitimately tried to give the human half of their bond a choice in their fate. I'd been so caught up in the fact that the humans who bonded were never going to be able to have children of their own that I'd lost sight of the fact that the gargoyles were facing the same problem.

Giving up kids seemed like one of those decisions that no eighteen-year-old should be allowed to make, but I supposed if there was an older person who was absolutely positive they never wanted to have offspring, under the right circumstances it might be okay for them to be bonded. Once they were that old, they probably understood what they were getting into.

"Are we okay, Dani? I understand if you feel like you can never forgive me for not telling you exactly what you were getting into by agreeing to take me to a convention and expose all of those poor girls to me, but if there's any way for you to get past that, I would really like for us to be friends again. I was kind of enjoying having a second friend."

I shook my head at him in exasperation. "Some rebel you turned out to be. I'm starting to realize why Jerek is the one with the piercing and you simply stop at wearing clothes his mother wouldn't approve of. Deep down inside, you're just as much of a conformist as the rest of us."

Caine frowned. "If I wasn't already in so much trouble I think I'd be mad at you for saying that. I'll have you know that I would've gotten a piercing, but I never quite got the hang of it."

"What do you mean you never quite got the hang of it? It's a piercing. They stick a needle through you and then thread metal through the hole. It doesn't seem like there's much to get the hang of."

"Says the girl who up until forty-eight hours ago didn't believe there was such a thing as gargoyles. When we're in pain, our bodies' natural resistance to damage kicks in. I went in two or three times in an attempt to get my eyebrow pierced, but I don't have good enough control over my abilities to keep my skin from hardening. Every time I've tried to get pierced, all I ended up doing was bending the needles they used on me. Jerek is one of the few gargoyles our age to have mastered his abilities well enough to actually get a piercing."

"So a piercing isn't just a sign of rebellion in your culture, it's also a sign of power and control."

It was yet another sign that Jerek wasn't the spoiled brat I'd originally thought, and more than ever I found myself wishing that I had a way of seeing inside his head and figuring out what made him tick. Caine gave me a knowing look that seemed to indicate he had at least some idea of where my thoughts were headed, but for once he didn't give me a hard time. His original question hung in the air between us for several more seconds before I sighed.

"Yeah, we're good. I'm not saying we're always going to be good—I reserve the right to never speak to you again if you charm some poor girl into giving up something she doesn't really want to give up, but until then it doesn't seem fair to hold something you haven't done against you."

Chapter 14

The rest of the flight was uneventful. Jerek remained up in the cockpit with Thomas, while Caine and I retreated back inside our respective psyches. Neither of us was mad at the other, but we'd simply gone through too much to sit there and yammer on about the weather. He needed time to pull himself back together after telling me what had happened to his parents, and I needed time to process all of the revelations he'd shared with me.

I was so lost inside of my own head that I didn't even realize we'd landed somewhere other than in Clay until I stepped off of the plane and scanned my surroundings.

"This isn't Clay."

Caine shook his head. "Nope. Jerek would never be stupid enough to land in Clay with his mom's goons in hot pursuit. We stole the fastest plane in her fleet, but that still didn't buy us enough time to get away from the airport once we landed before we would have a squad of heavy strike gargoyles surrounding us with their weapons drawn."

Jerek led Thomas down the stairs as Caine pulled me to the side. Now that we were away from Salt Lake, Jerek seemed less concerned about Thomas making a break for it, but he was still keeping a close eye on the older man.

"More like two squads at the very least. Actually, I'm hoping for a lot more than that. Mother was only willing to send out a squad of riven to check out Madeline Island before, but she's going to take Thomas' security a lot more seriously than unsubstantiated rumors of some kind of super-infestation of hunters. The last thing she wants to do is go back to being sterile again. She needs at least several more backups to her backups before she'll be confident that she can dispose of me and not have to worry about our family losing control of the kingdom."

Jerek made his statement with such calm acceptance that my heart went out to him. It would be hard to know that your parents valued you primarily as a way of continuing some kind of royal legacy. I opened my mouth with vague plans of trying to apologize for him having such crappy parents, but he didn't give me a chance.

"We're in Ashland, Wisconsin right now, which means that we're about half an hour's drive away from Clay. That means we should be able to get a boat and make it to the island not too much after dark."

The thought of running into more hunters when I couldn't even see what was stalking me didn't engender any kind of confidence. Even knowing that Jerek and Caine could see almost as well at night as they could during the day still didn't change the fact that I wouldn't be able to see anything.

"Are you sure that's a good idea?"

Caine reached over and grabbed my hand so he could spin me around as though we were dancing. "Don't worry about it, Dani. Night is the best time to go looking for hunters. That pale skin stands out like nobody's business. Plus, when you throw in the fact that Jerek's mom and all of the riven can fly, darkness makes even more sense. They'll be able to quarter all the islands and a big chunk of the mainland in very short order."

It was nice to see Caine reverting back to more of his usual easy manner after getting so somber on the flight to Ashland, but I wasn't quite sure the occasion was proper for dancing. Jerek seemed to agree with my assessment. I saw his mouth tighten when Caine grabbed my hand. The expression was gone by the time I completed my twirl and was looking his direction again, but his manner seemed more brusque than normal as he ordered Caine to go rent us a vehicle.

I watched as Thomas and Jerek talked to the ground crew in the hangar where we were parked, and then the two of them walked back over to where I was leaning against the plane. Jerek was being very careful to keep himself between Thomas and me still, which I appreciated, and I found myself wishing it was just the two of us so I could ask him some of the questions that were building up in the back of my mind.

Luckily, Jerek broke the silence first. "Is your wrist doing better now? You haven't been favoring it since we rescued Caine, but it looked like a pretty nasty sprain."

I reached down and touched my left wrist. I'd forgotten all about the spill back on the island that had sprained it, but it hadn't hurt for hours, in fact I couldn't remember feeling any pain since approximately when we'd touched and my emotions had been washed away.

"Actually, now that you mention it, my wrist feels fine now, which is odd. That should have hurt for weeks. It's like being around you and Caine is causing me to develop super powers. At this rate I'll be able to wipe the floor with Superman before the year is out."

I knew it was a weak joke, but I expected something more than the sympathy smile I got out of Jerek. He muttered something under his breath that I couldn't quite make out, but it sounded an awful lot like he said that things were moving much more quickly than he was expecting.

It didn't make any sense, but Jerek turned to go and I realized I might not get another chance to talk to him before we saw his mother again.

"I'm sorry if Caine and I got carried away. I know there's a lot at stake right now, and neither of us meant to act as though this was just some kind of spring break trip."

That was odd. I had dozens of questions I wanted to ask him, but instead of getting any of them out I'd apologized for how I'd been acting.

Jerek shook his head. "If anyone was to blame for that, it would be Caine. He's got a good heart. I know that he's told you about the way our society works, so you should be aware that if he does bond someone he'll be forced into the gargoyle equivalent of a marriage before the year is out. None of the nobility is allowed to shirk their responsibility with regards to replenishing our numbers."

It took me a second to realize what he was getting at, but as soon as I did I had to fight the urge to blush.

"It's not like that. My curse means that I've spent the last several years without any friends—guy or girl. That's all I want for Caine and me. He's easy to get along with and he seems like a really decent guy, but I just can't think of him as boyfriend material. Even if there wasn't such a big chance that he was going to end up bonded to some poor human girl and then subsequently married off to a gargoyle chick."

Jerek was silent for several seconds, but I got the sense that he was relieved. For a heartbeat or two I allowed myself to believe it was because Jerek was somehow interested in me, but I knew that wasn't the case. He'd never been anything but distant, which meant his relief simply had to do with the fact that he no longer had to worry I was going to break Caine's heart.

As we walked toward the main administration building where Caine was supposedly finding us a vehicle, I found myself casting around for something else to break the silence between us.

"How many brothers and sisters do you have?"

"I have five siblings, which sounds like a lot until you remember that we gargoyles are in the middle of the war and only a small percentage of our population base is able to reproduce."

"Are you close to any of them?"

Jerek was silent for so long that I almost thought he wasn't going to answer me. When he did finally speak there was a frosty undertone to his words.

"You don't need to do this, Dani."

"Do what?"

Jerek sighed. "Make small talk. You're along today because I didn't have anywhere safe to leave you while the rest of us dealt with the hunters, but it's not like you and I are going to become close friends once this is all over."

It took a lot to offend me, but Jerek had finally managed to do it. I stopped and put my hands on my hips.

"What is that supposed to mean? All I was trying to do was be nice, which is way more than you deserve based on the way you've treated me so far. Caine is convinced that you're a changed man, that you're no longer the stuck-up snob who used to idly watch while everyone tormented him, but I'm not so convinced. What exactly is your problem?"

Jerek's expression was all storm clouds and lightning, but his voice came out just as distant as it always did. "I can't explain everything that's going on, but suffice it to say that you and I can't be friends. In fact, you are probably the last person on earth I should be spending time with."

"Why? Because I'm human? So you're all about equality for someone like Caine—who the rest of your people despise simply because of who his parents were—but talking to a little human like me is a waste of oxygen? Look, let's do both of us a favor. Compel somebody to give me a ride home and neither of us ever has to see the other again."

"I won't waste time arguing with your erroneous assumptions. The truth is that the thought of never running into you again is one of the most desirable outcomes I can dream of, but things have progressed much too far for that. As I said before, my mother is not the kind to leave loose ends lying around.

"You came to her attention because of Caine and me, which means that it's my responsibility to make sure that you're able to live a long, free life. I will do my best to honor my obligation, but even if I don't make it out of the next few hours alive and un-incarcerated, then you'll need to stay close to Caine for at least the next several years. He's not as experienced at this kind of thing as would be ideal, but I've made arrangements in the event of my death, which should make sure that the two of you have a chance of staying out of my mother's grasp long enough for you to die of natural causes."

Jerek turned and walked away without another word. I watched him push Thomas along ahead of him for several seconds before I managed to force myself to follow along behind.

It had finally become obvious to me that it didn't matter whether Caine was right and Jerek was capable of caring about other people, or if he'd simply tricked Caine somehow. The simple fact of the matter was that Jerek despised me for no good reason that I could discern. I knew better than to throw myself at some guy who viewed me as nothing more than a burden, and even if I hadn't, the more I saw Jerek the less attracted to him I was.

STONE HEART

The only problem was that despite everything, some ridiculous part of me was still hung up on the idea that if I could just break through his shell everything would be different.

Seventeen years of life and I had to get hung up on one of only two guys in the world who were invulnerable to my curse. Too bad I'd picked the one who couldn't have cared less about me.

Chapter 15

The drive to the nearest marina was surprisingly short, and I found myself wondering why Jerek had even bothered having Caine rent a vehicle. It really would've been easier to just compel some poor airport employee to drop us off at the edge of the lake. The oddness didn't end when we got out of the rental SUV either. Jerek left Caine to keep an eye on Thomas and me while he went off and rented us a boat.

It was pretty obvious that he was doing his best to spend as little time around me as possible, but apparently Caine wasn't quite as perceptive as I'd given him credit for. Actually, that made quite a bit of sense given the fact that Jerek had convinced him that the heir to the gargoyle throne was something other than a stuck-up, spoiled brat.

Caine kept looking back and forth between Jerek and me as though trying to figure out what was going on, but I wasn't about to be the first one to break the silence between us. If Caine wanted to know why things had gotten so tense, then he needed to ask Jerek. I was perfectly happy to pretend like we were all still one big happy family.

Once we were all loaded into the boat, Jerek turned Thomas' phone back on and dialed his mother. This time he left the phone on speaker so I didn't have any problem hearing what was being said.

"It appears that you filed a fraudulent flight plan."

"Yes, I did. It was the only way to make sure that you actually went out to Madeline Island rather than just intercepting us at the airport. I assume you're already in town?"

"Of course we're in town. We arrived fifteen minutes ago just as the sun started to set, and I've already got a full squad of my people out scouting for this supposed infestation of hunters. Now where is Thomas?"

Jerek's mother sounded beyond pissed, but he didn't seem worried. "He's with us, and he'll stay with us until I'm satisfied your people have made an honest attempt to find the hunters. We'll meet you at the house on Madeline Island in a little while."

Jerek hung up on his mother, but this time he didn't power the phone off. Caine gave him a questioning look as he started the engine on the boat, but Jerek apparently wasn't opposed to answering his best friend's questions.

"There isn't a whole lot of reason trying to make sure she can't track us at this point. The riven aren't likely to try and pull Thomas out of the boat while we're on the water."

Caine pushed off from the dock and a few seconds later we were underway, but unlike the last boating trip we'd been on, Jerek didn't seem to be in a hurry to get where we were going. We motored off at no more than five or ten miles an hour, and I settled in for a long trip.

It was fully dark by the time we'd been on the water for another twenty minutes, and I was starting to get a little freaked out. Caine and Jerek might have excellent night vision, but to me it looked like we were headed through darkness so thick that even a pair of gargoyles couldn't possibly navigate safely. I told myself I was worrying about nothing, but I was still nervous enough that I jumped several inches out of my seat when Thomas' phone started ringing.

Jerek answered the phone without throttling back the engine. "Did you find them yet?"

"Not only have we not found them, we haven't even found the bodies of the ones you claimed to have killed before you left your post to come to Salt Lake. So far there hasn't been even the slightest sign that the portal is active. All of the major factories and other enterprises in this area have continued to function as normal. My IT assets are coming up completely blank. No missed shipments, no uptick in employee absences or paid time off, nothing to indicate that we've got a nest of hunters trying to build their strength up to the point where they can bring an elder over to this side of the portal."

"That's impossible. Are your people really looking? They can't just fly over and expect to sniff this group out like they normally do. They're going to have to actually use their eyes and do some real detective work."

Jerek sounded worried, which just seemed to make his mother switch from angry to satisfied. "Of course they're looking. Despite the fact that everyone with me thinks your super-hunters are just as unlikely as I think they are, I ordered them to pretend for the time being that your theories were valid. If there was really a batch of hunters on this side of the portal we would've found them by now. Now quit stalling and get your butt over here. I'm not going to just sweep this under the rug. You've finally done something egregious enough that even your father won't fight me when it comes to punishing you."

"I refuse to believe that there were only those three hunters. You're not looking hard enough, and if you think I'm handing Thomas over before I'm fully satisfied that the infestation in this area has been found and contained, you're severely mistaken. Tell your scouts to run the search pattern again."

"I know exactly where you are, Jerek. What's to stop me from sending in a flight of flyers to take Thomas off of your boat?"

"The fact that I will happily wrap my arms around him as I jump out into the water and drag him down to the bottom of the lake. That's the funny thing about telling someone that you're going to execute them even if they turn themselves in. It means they don't have any reason to meet you halfway. Tell them to run it again or your current pregnancy will be your last."

Jerek hung up again and tried to pretend he wasn't rattled by the fact that nobody had managed to find any hunters yet, but even I could tell that he hadn't expected for things to come to this.

Thomas, who was sitting at the front of the boat with Caine positioned between him and me, tried to make a case for Jerek turning himself in sooner rather than later. He even tried to claim that he would put a good word in for Jerek with the queen, but we all knew that promise wasn't worth anything. As soon as the queen told Thomas to cut Jerek's throat, he would do it without a second thought about the fact that he was violating his sworn word. He didn't have a choice in the matter, but it didn't change the fact that he couldn't be trusted.

I tried to imagine what it would be like to grow up knowing that your parents had foisted you off onto a human who was taking care of you primarily because they didn't have any other option. It seemed like a recipe for a pretty terrible childhood, and I once again found myself wanting to give Jerek the benefit of the doubt.

Growing up with distant parents and a guardian who would happily stick you in a bag and drown you if that was what your parents wanted, was the kind of thing that led people to becoming psychopaths. I kept telling myself that Jerek's past didn't excuse his current treatment of me, but no matter how many times I told myself that, it still seemed like my indictment of him rang hollow even to me.

I wasn't used to being this conflicted about anyone, let alone a guy who was completely uninterested in me. It wasn't a very comfortable feeling, and despite the fact that I knew it was probably bad news, I felt a surge of relief when the phone rang again half an hour later.

"What did they find?"

Jerek still seemed like he was trying to sound nonplussed, but the facade was cracking with every passing second. Even his mother seemed to have a pretty good idea of just how badly he'd cornered himself.

"Exactly the same thing as we found the first time around. I've even had my hackers analyze satellite surveillance over this area for the last six weeks. Even the traffic patterns don't show so much as a blip. If there are hunters in this area, not only do they not give off the distinctive smell that was a signature characteristic of every hunter we've encountered for the last seven thousand years, they've also restrained themselves to the point where none of their victims have been forced to miss any work, and they haven't even been using the humans as chauffeurs to get from point to point. In short, if there's a nest of hunters in Wisconsin, they're acting so far outside of their normal operational patterns that I'm not sure they can even legitimately be called hunters anymore."

"Why is that so hard to believe? We know that they're smart. We've seen them hunt down our noncombatants and ambush our patrols, is this really that much of a departure from that?"

"No, they're cunning. There's a difference, and even their cunning shows up in direct proportion to how many elders there are in the area. By themselves, an individual hunter isn't even as smart as a water buffalo, and you and I both know there's no way that we've got a full-blown elder on this side of the portal anywhere within two hundred miles of here. Elders are cunning, but they're even less inclined toward self-restraint than the rest of their kind. If there was an elder here, the National Guard would have already been called in to try to quell violence the likes of which this country has never seen."

Jerek slumped forward in his seat as though finally admitting defeat. "Very well, we'll be arriving at the house within the next five minutes. You can go ahead and call your people back."

Caine barely waited until Jerek had hung up the phone before he started protesting. "Going to the house is suicide, and you know it. Your mom can't possibly allow something like this to stand. A threat to Thomas is a threat to her, and no monarch lasts long once they start letting people threaten their own safety. We need to turn around and make a run for it."

Jerek shook his head. "No, I considered that, but we wouldn't make it five miles. As long as we're on the water, Mother won't come after us simply because none of her people can swim any better than you or me. We can't stay here forever though, and once we get to dry land, all bets are off. Our only chance is to go back to the island and use Thomas as a bargaining chip."

"No, that won't work either. She won't like it, but your mother will risk injuring Thomas if that's what is required to take the rest of us down."

"You're right. Mother can't afford to let me get away, but if we tell her that you and Dani wanted no part of my plan, that you were just along because I threatened to hurt Thomas if you didn't do exactly as I said, then there's a chance she'll let me trade myself for your freedom. She'll know that you were in this up to your eyeballs, but you and Dani are small potatoes in comparison to making sure that I'm out of the picture for good."

Caine looked like he wanted to break some-thing, and I was surprised to realize I was nearly as angry about the situation as he was. "You told me you weren't just going to lie down and let your mother execute you. That's the only reason I went along with this harebrained idea of yours."

"I know. I knew you wouldn't agree to any of this unless you thought I had a way out in the event my suspicions about the hunters were wrong. That's why I lied to you. I'm sorry, Caine, but it had to be done, and now that things are falling apart, you don't have any choice but to go along with my plan. Sacrificing yourself won't save me, and it will guarantee that Dani either gets executed alongside the two of us or imprisoned somewhere until she dies of old age. She doesn't deserve that, and you know it."

"It won't work. Thomas will never agree to keep his mouth shut, and even if he did, one word from your mother and he'll be spilling all the details of your master plan."

Jerek reached into one of the compartments next to the driver's seat and fished out an oversized roll of duct tape. "You're right, but I already thought of a way around that. If we duct-tape him so he can't move or speak, then he won't have a chance to spill the beans. That means all I have to do is put my back to a wall, wrap my hands around his neck, and then stand Mommy dearest off for long enough to give the two of you a nice, fat, head start. It's not going to be as long as you would like, but I ought to be able to bluff everyone back at the house for at least an hour or two. That should be enough time for you to get to a big enough city that you have a chance of losing any pursuit. Just be smart and don't take any unnecessary risks. There's every reason to believe that the two of you could die free individuals having lived out full lives."

"I don't like it."

Despite everything my mouth was halfway open to echo Caine's sentiment, but Jerek cut me off with a stern glance. "I don't like it either, but this was my choice. I got the two of you into this mess, and it's only fair that I do whatever I can to get you out of it. Let me do this for the two of you. Please."

Caine refused to answer for nearly a minute, but eventually Jerek's unflinching gaze forced a single, choppy nod out of him. I expected that to be the end of the discussion, but Jerek wasn't satisfied until I'd also agreed to let him sacrifice himself to buy us time to escape.

As Jerek throttled the boat back up and turned us so we were headed directly to Madeline Island, I tried to sort out the conflicting tide of emotions inside me. How was I supposed to reconcile my image of a selfish prince who thought humans were some kind of lesser life form with a man who seemed determined to sacrifice himself to buy my freedom?

Chapter 16

We arrived at the dock below Jerek's house far too quickly for me to figure out what exactly I was feeling, but at least I wasn't as physically uncomfortable as Thomas was. Jerek hadn't been kidding when he said he was going to duct-tape his old caregiver, and he hadn't stopped just with putting a strip of tape over Thomas' mouth.

Jerek had started at Thomas' shoulders and wrapped loops of tape all the way down to his wrists so that the old man was forced to stand with his arms straight along his sides. Jerek had threatened to latch onto Thomas as a way of pulling them down to the bottom of the lake, but the truth was that with the way Thomas' arms were trapped at his sides, Jerek wouldn't need to jump into the water with them to ensure that his mother's pet human would drown.

Just thinking about dying that way, slowly sinking underneath the surface of the water, powerless to break free of the restraints that were stopping me from swimming, was enough to give me nightmares so I focused instead on all of the angry-looking men and women gathered around the perimeter of Jerek's house. Jerek had been right when he'd said that the queen wouldn't travel into a potentially danger-ous situation without a full complement of guards.

The four riven who'd been serving as our guards back in Salt Lake were there, but I didn't recognize anyone else among the more than two dozen weapon-wielding soldiers who were glaring at us as we made our way up the stairs to the house. We made an awkward-looking procession with Thomas in the front, Jerek's hands around his throat, then me with Caine at my back to protect me in case the queen ordered one of her people to take me out from afar. It was slow going, but I felt a lot safer knowing that I was sandwiched between two gargoyles who were capable of turning their skin into something harder than granite.

I'd been half expecting for the four of us to be ushered inside the house, but apparently Jerek was no longer welcome at home anymore. The queen was waiting for us in the pool area as we made it to the top of the stairs.

"I see that you finally decided to stop stalling. Release Thomas and I'll make your death a painless one."

"Hello, Mother. It's nice to see you, too. You brought all these people here just for little old me? I must say I'm flattered. There was a time when you wouldn't have doubted your ability to take me out all by yourself."

"I still could, but given the fact that you have Thomas by the throat it seemed prudent to make sure that killing you didn't become some kind of long drawn-out affair."

Jerek had continued moving while he was talking, and by the time their exchange ended, he was standing with his back to a massive tree at the edge of the patio area.

"Here's the deal, Mother. Dani and Caine went along with my plan under protest. They did what they did only because they were worried that I would go through with my threat to kill Thomas. I'm going to turn myself in and release Thomas, but only if they are granted full pardons."

"You don't actually expect me to believe that, do you?"

I'd forgotten all about the fact that the queen was able to tell when someone was lying to her, but based on Jerek's cold smile he hadn't. "I don't know, is the life of your pet human important to you? Before you tell me that I'm not in a position to negotiate, let me remind you that I am perfectly willing to kill Thomas if that's what is required to secure the freedom of two people who've done nothing wrong."

The queen considered that statement for several seconds as though weighing the truth behind his words and then waved negligently. "Very well, they have pardons. Now let Thomas go."

"Of course, as soon as the two of them are safely out of your reach. Instruct your people to allow them to depart. Two hours from now, once both they and I are satisfied that they haven't been followed, I will release Thomas and you can do with me as you wish."

Jerek's mother shook her head. "They will be staying here. I want them to witness the penalty for this kind of treachery. They can go after they've seen you die."

"If you want them to see my execution then have one of your henchmen film it. The only reason for you to refuse my terms is if you're not actually planning on pardoning them. You have thirty seconds to call off your dogs or I'll just snap Thomas' neck and take my chance with a weapon in my hands."

It was like watching two demigods trying to stare each other down. I would've backed down within seconds if it had been me on the opposite end of either of those stares, but neither of them so much as blinked as Jerek's deadline wound down. There was no telling what would've happened next if all hell hadn't broken loose precisely five seconds before Jerek had said he was going to execute Thomas.

Between one heartbeat and the next several dozen hunters materialized out of the darkness and attacked the queen's warriors. As badly as it seemed that Jerek and his mother hated each other, neither of them hesitated in the slightest once their common enemy showed up.

Jerek pushed Thomas towards the center of the pool area at the same time that Caine pulled me towards the queen. I nearly fell into the pool, but managed to catch my balance and spin around in time to see Jerek slam the head of his hammer into a hunter who was at least three inches taller and forty pounds heavier than the one I'd seen him kill just days earlier.

Watching Jerek fight off just one hunter had been scary, but that was nothing compared to this. The gargoyles were badly outnumbered, and the hunters seemed to have taken them completely by surprise. Everyone had been focused on Jerek rather than trying to maintain any kind of secure perimeter, and that meant we lost more than half a dozen gargoyles just in the opening few seconds of the fight.

The survivors rallied with impressive determination, but now they were even more badly outnumbered, and even the extra reach granted by their weapons didn't look to me like it was going to be enough to offset our numerical disadvantage. I watched as Caine knocked one set of claws away with the long daggers he'd taken from the house in Salt Lake, but before he could capitalize on the opening he'd just created, another hunter landed a blow to his shoulder that skittered away in a shower of sparks.

Caine's skin seemed to have turned the blow, but I knew he could only rely on his body's natural resistance to damage for so long before it would fail him. The force of the attack that had just landed knocked Caine backwards more than six feet, but he flared out black, bat-like wings to stop his backwards momentum and then slammed the point of one of his daggers into the throat of the closest hunter.

It was an impressive recovery—the kind of thing that happened so fast I almost couldn't follow it—but I was able to see it for what it really was. It wasn't luck, that wouldn't have been giving Caine enough credit, but I knew his skill wasn't sufficient to guarantee he could replicate that kind of quick, instant kill over and over again while fighting two or even three hunters at a time.

Everywhere I looked more of the same kind of desperate fighting met my eyes. It looked like the queen had brought representatives from all three branches of the guard, and the scouts did seem to be getting the worst of it, but even the heavy strike warriors looked like they were fighting a losing battle. As I watched, three more gargoyles went reeling backwards bleeding from wounds that their stone-hard skin hadn't been able to turn.

It looked like our guys had managed to kill seven or eight of the hunters in return, but that wasn't enough to begin reversing the odds against us.

I wanted to make a run for the house, or barring that, to curl up in a little ball next to the swimming pool, but something inside of me refused to let me do that while surrounded by so many brave fighters. It was obvious to me that none of us were going to make it out alive, but none of the queen's men even flinched.

Instead of giving up, I headed forward, planning on grabbing a weapon from one of the gargoyles bleeding to death next to the pool, but before I could make it to my destination a massive crash from behind me brought me around to see that there was one place where the battle wasn't going completely against us.

Caine had told me that Jerek was a much better fighter once he had a weapon in his hand, but even that hadn't prepared me for what I was seeing now. Jerek was fighting three hunters at the same time and winning. He swung the massive metal hammer that was nearly as tall as I was like it weighed nothing, and moved with the kind of speed and grace that not even the other heavy strike warriors seemed to be able to match.

Over just the course of a couple seconds I saw Jerek materialize his wings for just long enough to bat away a strike that otherwise would've opened up the entire right side of his chest. The wings disappeared just as quickly as they'd materialized, but they did the job of deflecting the attack, which left Jerek free to slam his hammer into the side of another hunter's head a split second before he used the haft of his weapon to stab a third enemy in the gut with enough force to pick it up and send it flying backwards for more than a dozen feet.

Jerek wasn't just deadly, he was a force of nature, and for the briefest of seconds I thought maybe he would be able to turn the tide for us. That hope lasted just until the gargoyle on the other side of him fell in a spray of blood and Jerek's opponents were joined by three more hunters.

The creature Jerek had bashed in the head looked dead, but the one he'd hit in the stomach had already bounced back to its feet and not even Jerek was capable of fighting off five hunters at the same time. I saw Caine trying to fall back to where he could support Jerek, but he was already obviously struggling against the two hunters he was faced off against. They were both bigger and obviously stronger and faster than the ones Caine had held off back at the marina, and I could tell it was only a matter of time before they were going to manage to get past his defenses and kill him.

Just when I thought that there was no hope left, a sheet of hot blue fire shot out of Jerek's mom's fingers and wrapped itself around a group of three hunters. An attack like that would've left nothing more than a pile of ash behind if it had managed to hit me, but the hunters were obviously made out of much sterner stuff than us poor humans.

The fire was burning them, but it seemed to be struggling to get any kind of real purchase on their flesh. All three fell back in an attempt to get out of the line of fire, which bought the closest gargoyle a second to breathe, but the reaction out of the rest of the hunters was unnerving. Almost as one, they let out a bloodcurdling scream and then threw themselves forward, heedless of the fact that doing so left them exposed to attacks from Jerek and the others.

The queen had said that the hunters weren't smart—just cunning—but what I saw in that instant seemed to indicate otherwise. The hunters had been intent on trying to kill all of us, but as soon as they realized that the queen was bonded, they went after her as though fully aware that killing her would prevent the birth of additional gargoyles.

Thomas had fallen to the ground, but rather than remaining motionless he'd rolled over to one of the fallen gargoyles and seemed to be trying to work a knife free of its belt. Everything came back to me in a flash and I hurried over to help. Thomas might not be as effective as a gargoyle, but if he was able to shoot fire out of his hands like the queen had just done, then there was a chance he could turn the tide of the battle.

I grabbed the knife he'd been struggling to get into play as the queen shot out additional tendrils of fire in an attempt to beat back the press of sickly white bodies. The gargoyles, Jerek and Caine included, had fallen back into a smaller perimeter in an effort to keep the hunters away from the queen, but doing so meant that they had a lot less room in which to dodge.

The gargoyles were all taking a lot more hits than they had been just a few seconds earlier, and the sheer number of hunters pressing in on them meant that a lot of their weapons were much less effective than they'd been previously. The gargoyles weilding stabbing weapons, like spears and even some of the thinner swords, were still managing to score some good hits, but they were the only ones, and there weren't enough of them. Anyone with a blunt weapon, like Jerek's hammer, or slashing weapons, like the big, two-handed swords that were favored by so many of the gargoyles, was struggling.

As I began cutting the duct tape away from Thomas' arms, Jerek thrust the head of his hammer forward, knocking one of the hunters back a couple of feet, but the blow was a weak shadow of what he'd managed back when he'd had room to swing the hammer the way it'd been intended to be wielded.

The queen's fire attacks already seemed to be weakening, and she unlimbered a heavy ax with one hand as I finally managed to get one of Thomas' arms free. I expected him to blast the closest hunter with a white-hot torrent of fire, but now that he was free he seemed to be at a loss for what to do next.

Before I could really process the fact that I'd just wasted precious time trying to free someone who was going to be completely useless, the queen yelled out an order.

"Listen to the girl! Let her choose your targets, Thomas."

Thomas looked at me expectantly with the kind of blind loyalty that I was more accustomed to seeing out of puppies than grown men old enough to be my father. I pointed at a hunter that had just dropped one of the heavy strike gargoyles and was working its way around to strike at Jerek's flank, and a second later Thomas cut loose with a tendril of fire. It was only a fraction of the size of what the queen had been capable of, but it still bored into the hunter with enough ferocity that the creature fell backwards and began rolling on the ground in an attempt to put out the flames.

I picked out another target, one that was causing Caine problems, as the Queen stepped to the edge of the circle and joined in the fighting. Everything Caine had told me about bonded gargoyles was absolutely true. The riven gargoyles had been faster and stronger than anyone—except for maybe Jerek—but they'd been the focus of some of the most severe fighting, so I'd gotten a good sense of just what they were capable of before they'd been cut down.

As deadly as they'd been, Jerek's mother had them beat. She stepped into the fray with an ax clenched in her hands and fire billowing around her. Her clothes disappeared instantly, but the fire wreathing her body preserved her modesty much better than the tattered clothes worn by the rest of the gargoyles. I hadn't expected the fire to make much of a difference given just how weak her last few attacks had been, but apparently projecting fire over a distance was much harder than what she was doing now.

The fire around her burned hot enough that I could feel it clawing at me from more than two dozen yards away, and the hunters were practically falling over each other in an attempt to get back out of range of her ax.

For a moment I thought we were saved. The Queen cut down three hunters in quick succession, and the very existence of the fire around her pushed back her enemies enough that Jerek and the others were able to exploit the opening to begin using their weapons the way they'd been meant to be wielded.

Thomas used his rapidly dying tendrils of fire to drive back another pair of hunters who were trying to work their way around to where they would be able to get at the two of us, and then Caine was falling back to help protect us. Everything looked like it was under control right up until a new hunter, one that was nearly eight feet tall, materialized out of the darkness and slammed his fist into the side of the queen's head.

It all happened so fast that I would've missed it if I hadn't been looking at exactly the right spot, and even then I had a hard time believing that my eyes weren't deceiving me. There was only one explanation for what I'd just seen, only one kind of hunter was capable of taking down even a bonded gargoyle all by itself.

Jerek and his mother had both been wrong. This wasn't just an infestation that was a few dozen hunters further along than anyone had believed possible, this was an infestation that included a full-blown elder, one who was powerful enough that he was able to shrug off the heat from the queen's fire in the split second it took him to disable her and kill the fire.

The gargoyles were all just as shocked as I was, and for a moment everyone paused as they tried to adjust to the appearance of the one enemy nobody had expected to fight. The hunters could've used our side's shock to cut down half of the remaining gargoyles, but they'd likewise moved back out of engagement range as soon as the elder revealed himself.

I was actually proud of the fact that I recovered before anyone else did. Maybe it was simply that all of this was so unbelievable already that the addition of a hunter elder that none of us had been expecting to fight wasn't as much of an intellectual jump for me as it was for everyone else, but I slapped Thomas in the arm as I pointed to the elder.

"Hit it with everything you've got left!"

Thomas responded instantly with a blast of fire nearly as powerful as what the queen had been manifesting when she'd first joined the fray. I was well back behind Thomas when he took his shot at the elder, and I still half expected my clothes to spontaneously combust from the heat, but the elder shrugged off the attack like it was nothing.

The two closest gargoyles threw themselves at the elder with a fury that told me their loyalty to the queen was more than loyalty in name only. I could see the elder's skin blackening and then instantly healing under the assault of Thomas' jet of fire, but that didn't even seem to slow it down as it slammed its claws into the chest of the first gargoyle and then broke the neck of the second.

After the sustained violence of just the last few minutes, I felt like nothing should've been able to shock me anymore, but the ease with which the hunter elder dispatched the two gargoyles left me stunned. The one who had been stabbed in the chest had been wearing clothes that were remarkably undamaged, so I'd been expecting him to be able to at least turn one attack, but apparently the elder was capable of striking with such force that even a gargoyle's natural resistance to damage wasn't enough to deflect those cruel claws.

In that moment I realized that there was nothing any of us could do to stop the elder from killing us all, but rather than capitalize on the situation, the hunter elder backed away with a hiss.

"Kill them all."

As the elder disappeared with Jerek's mother slung over his shoulder, her blood trickling down his back, I kept expecting Thomas to die as a result of the bond being severed, but he simply looked at me blankly, as though unable to comprehend what had just happened. Despite the fact that Thomas was far too old to need comforting, I wanted to wrap my arms around his waist and tell him that everything would be okay. Before I could get a word out the hunters resumed their attack, and we no longer had any surprises to pull out of our collective sleeves.

Jerek had been only seconds away from being executed as a traitor when the hunters had arrived on the scene, but now that his mother had been carried away, he was our side's most deadly warrior and the rest of our people formed around him, guarding his back as he tried to carry the fight to the hunters. He continued to swing his massive silver hammer as though it weighed just ounces, but despite the grace and power in his movements I could see that he was as outmatched as the rest of us.

I looked down at my right hand and realized that I was still holding the knife I'd used to cut Thomas free of the duct tape, and found myself wondering if a weapon that small was even capable of killing a hunter. We lost two more gargoyles in short order, and I realized that I was about to find out.

The ring around Thomas, Caine, and me had shrunk down to the point where there was less than a dozen feet between Jerek and me, and it continued to contract from a combination of the sheer weight of the hunters' numbers, and our ongoing losses. It seemed as though the fragile line of fighting gargoyles would break at any moment, and then Jerek somehow managed to reverse the momentum of the battle enough to take a step forward rather than continuing to retreat.

Jerek's advance wasn't without cost. I could see blood streaming out of five or six different gashes on his body, but each swing of his hammer dispatched another hunter, and he shrugged off the damage he was absorbing as simply another cost of doing business. I'd never seen anything as heroic, but even as a wave of admiration crashed through me, I knew that nobody could withstand that kind of battering for long.

As the gargoyle to Jerek's right went down in a spray of blood, and Jerek spun to the side to dispatch his comrade's killer, I finally realized what it was that Jerek was trying to accomplish. He was trying to work his way back over to the massive tree he'd been counting on guarding his back while he stood off his mother's warriors.

I pulled Thomas into motion as Caine stumbled towards his friend in an attempt to watch his right flank, but I could tell that none of us were going to be quick enough. Things had been happening with such speed that I hadn't been able to follow any more than just flickers of action as it occurred around me, but the scream that sounded behind me a split second later was more ominous than anything else I'd heard so far that night.

It was dangerous to look away from the tree that was our goal, but I couldn't help but turn to see what was happening behind me. As soon as my mind made sense of what I was seeing I wished that I'd successfully battled the urge. The gargoyles who'd been fighting so valiantly on the other side of the ring from Jerek to protect Thomas and me had fallen, and the tide of hunters was headed towards us with the kind of blinding speed I knew I couldn't match.

I knew I was going to die, and there was nothing I could do about it. I pushed Thomas on ahead of me in the hopes that he at least would be able to make it to the safety of the tree, and then turned so I was facing the hunters.

It was foolish—there was no way I was a match for even one of the creatures, let alone three—but that didn't stop me from hefting the knife in my right hand as I backpedaled in an attempt to buy myself an extra heartbeat or two of life. A split second before the closest hunter would've been able to sink its claws into me, someone grabbed me by the shoulder and hurled me backwards like I weighed barely anything at all.

Jerek's hammer slammed into the hunter who'd been about to kill me and crushed its chest. As his weapon rebounded off of his latest victim, Jerek tried to spin around enough to interpose the haft of his weapon so that it could stop the next attack headed at him, but somewhere along the way he'd lost half a step. He was no longer fast enough to get away with something that reckless.

The bloody wounds marring Jerek's body were nothing compared to what happened next, and I winced for him as I saw four long claws take him in the right side of the chest. The hunter stabbed him and then ripped its claws free in a spray of blood. Jerek went down on one knee as though no longer possessed of the strength to stand on his own, but then Caine arrived at his side. Caine dragged Jerek to his feet with one hand and then sent a knife sailing end over end through the air to lodge itself in the throat of one of the hunters.

All of that took only a fraction of a second, so I was still falling backwards as Caine pulled Jerek back in my direction. The impact as my butt hit the ground should've left me curled up in a ball trying not to sob while I waited for the pain to go away, but there was simply too much adrenaline coursing through my body for something like that to even register inside my mind.

I hit the ground and practically bounced back to my feet as I spun around to make sure that I wouldn't run headlong into the tree. Thomas was already there, his fire mostly spent, save for a watermelon-sized ball of flame cupped in his left hand. I knew that wouldn't be enough to stop even a single hunter, but I had some hope that it would serve as a deterrent—right up until I realized that there was only one gargoyle standing next to the tree with Thomas.

I'd known we were losing warriors, but somehow I hadn't realized just how many we'd lost. As Jerek and Caine arrived at the tree and stood only inches away from me, I surveyed our surroundings and wanted to cry at what I saw.

There were dead and dying gargoyles scattered throughout the pool area like broken toys, and the greater number of dead hunters was small consolation in the face of just how many hunters still remained alive. Jerek and the others had trimmed down the number of enemies that we'd been facing, but seeing that there were only five of them left was small consolation given that we were still outnumbered, and Thomas and I were the only two on our side who weren't losing dangerous amounts of blood.

"You're going to need to make a run for it, Dani."

Jerek spoke so quietly that I almost didn't realize he was talking to me, and even then I only heard him because the hunters were standing just outside of the reach of the gargoyles' weapons.

"I'm not leaving you."

"You don't belong here, Dani. This is the last place I ever wanted you to be. I failed in my attempt to keep you safe, but there's still a chance for you to make it out of here alive. The hunters outnumber us, but it looks like they're going to try to wait us out and see if simple blood loss will do their job for them. We're going to have to carry the fight to them while I still have the strength to walk. When that happens, I want you to make a break for the boat."

My mind was spinning so fast I almost couldn't get it to put together complete thoughts. Fragments of what Jerek had said were lodged inside of my mind like shards of shrapnel, but they stubbornly refused to form any kind of coherent narrative.

What did he mean, he'd been trying to keep me safe? The obvious answer was that he'd been trying to get Caine and me safely away from his mother, but something about his voice seemed to indicate there was more to it than just that. I fixated on the one thought that had made it through before my mind had decided it no longer wanted to function.

"I don't even know how to get the boat started, Jerek. Not only that, I would have to untie the ropes holding it to the dock before I could even get moving. You and I both know I'm not going to have that kind of time, but none of that matters because I'm not running away and leaving you all to die. If you want to save me, then figure out a way to kill the rest of those hunters."

"Jerek's right, Dani. You don't belong here—I never should have gotten you involved in our world. You're right too, though. I don't see how you have any chance of making it to the boat by yourself before the hunters catch up with you. We need another plan."

Caine had produced another dagger from somewhere, and he tapped the hilt against Jerek's shoulder as though testing just how hard his friend's skin still was. "What about your wings? Could you grab Dani while the rest of us created a distraction and fly to the boats? You're a heck of a lot better with those things than you have any business to be. Now seems like the perfect time to use them."

Jerek shook his head. "It'll never work. I've lost too much strength to manifest them now, and even if that wasn't the case they're too unpredictable. I only use them when I don't have any other choice, and I've been lucky that they haven't let me down so far."

"There's something more than luck going on. I saw you fighting with them, and I've never seen anything like it out of someone who wasn't bonded. I don't suppose you'd be willing to tell me how you're managing that little trick. You know, as my dying request from one friend to another?"

"Sorry, I don't know what's going on there any more than you do. They just started working more reliably a little while ago for no reason."

My mind still seemed to be skipping, but I was very much convinced that Jerek had just lied, and that didn't seem like him at all—not when we were all going to die so soon. I opened my mouth to call him on his deception, but before I could say anything the hunters decided that they'd waited long enough.

Acting in unison on some kind of unseen signal, all five of them sprang forward. The third gargoyle, the one standing by Thomas, went down as a set of claws opened him up from hip to collarbone, but Thomas managed to slam his burning hand into the hunter that had just killed his last bodyguard, and the bodyguard stabbed a second hunter through the stomach as he went down.

That meant that Jerek and Caine were only facing three hunters. Under other circumstances, I was almost positive that Jerek could have easily killed all three hunters himself, but given just how much blood was streaming down his side, I was pretty sure it was all he could do to remain standing.

Caine had his one remaining dagger tucked back along his right forearm where it would be used to block or attack either one, but I could tell by the set of his shoulders that he knew the two of them didn't have any chance of surviving. He stepped forward into the closest hunter as Jerek's massive hammer crashed into the hunter in the middle, but both of their efforts were insufficient for the task at hand.

Jerek's hammer hit the target he'd been aiming at, but he was too unsteady to generate any kind of real force with the blow. Rather than sending the hunter flying with crushed limbs and broken bones, the attack barely even staggered the hunter, who grabbed the haft of Jerek's hammer before it could finish recoiling away.

Caine scored a slash to the outside of his opponent's arm, but before he could recover from his strike, the hunter drove its claws deep into his gut, and he went down in a spray of blood. I wanted to help—I even took a step forward in an attempt to get my little knife into play—but everyone there knew that I wasn't a match for a hunter.

I'd been hoping against all hope that Jerek still had one more trick up his sleeve, but as the hunter who'd grabbed hold of his hammer ripped it away from him, I realized that wasn't the case. If Jerek still had anything in reserve he would've dusted it off already. We were all going to die, and there was nothing any of us could do about it.

STONE HEART

The hunter that had just taken Jerek's weapon away from him slammed the butt of his weapon into his stomach and then lashed out with razor-sharp claws that tore through the right side of Jerek's chest like it was made out of nothing more than tissue paper.

The tide of emotion that swept over me as Jerek started falling was so powerful that I had a hard time identifying individual feelings. It wasn't until Jerek turned his head so he could see me in the final instant before he hit the ground that I was finally able to understand what it was that I could feel coursing through me.

It was the sheer unexpectedness of Jerek choosing to look at me in his last moments that finally threw everything into clarity. I'd been expecting him to go down fighting, to die with his eyes fixed on the hunter trying to kill him, but in that moment I finally had proof that there was more to Jerek than he'd yet revealed to me.

There were plenty of reasons to be mad at our situation and the hunters that had trapped us there so we could be executed. More than two dozen gargoyles had died already, Thomas would be joining them in a moment, and for all I knew Caine had already bled to death, but for some reason none of that was the source of the white-hot rage trying to consume me from the inside out.

It felt like I was a cup that someone had poured molten metal into, only instead of cooling with the passage of each second, my rage begged to be used. I brandished my knife—useless though it was—and opened my mouth, intending on screaming out my defiance as our enemies killed Jerek and me. What happened next took everyone by surprise.

No sound came roaring out of my open mouth. Instead a torrent of fire every bit as powerful as anything the queen had demonstrated, rushed out in a white-hot blaze that consumed the hunter standing above Jerek in the split second before I twisted my head to the side to redirect the fire at the next hunter and then the next after that.

It was like I'd become a dragon, one powered by fury that exceeded anything I'd known I was capable of feeling.

The last hunter, the one standing over Thomas, was stronger than the rest and I had to burn him for several seconds before he finally ran away, the sole survivor of the group that had come within fractions of a second of killing the rest of our group. I sagged backwards against the tree that Jerek had been hoping would allow him to stand off our enemies for a few seconds longer, as I realized that I felt oddly hollow inside.

The cup full of molten rage was still there, but the terrifying energy I'd been feeling had been dissipated by my impossible destruction of the hunters. I could still feel the last dregs of the alien energy at the bottom of the cup, but I could tell that there was no longer sufficient anger inside me to power another burst of fire like the one I'd just used. I was too shocky to process the meaning of everything that had happened, but any question as to whether or not the energy was gone forever was answered as I felt the tiniest trickle of new anger begin the slow process of refilling my inner vessel.

Whatever had happened to me was a permanent change. I was now just as much a part of this impossible world as Jerek, Caine, or any of the rest of their race.

If I'd just been there by myself there was no way of knowing how long I would've sat there in stunned silence, but fortunately I wasn't by myself. Jerek was still losing blood at an alarming rate, but he somehow found the strength to turn over onto his stomach and begin crawling toward me.

"Dani, are you okay?"

That brought me back to myself enough to register just how close to death Jerek was. "I don't know what to do, Jerek. You're bleeding—a lot. How do I stop it?"

Jerek weakly coughed as he turned his head to the side far enough to confirm that Thomas was uninjured. "I'll be okay if I can just make it to the boat and drop into a healing trance before I lose enough blood to actually kill me. Get Thomas and have him help you carry Caine down to the boat. I think he's in a healing trance already, but we can't afford to stay here. One of the hunters got away, and even if he hadn't, there's no telling how soon the elder will be back to check on things. Unless we can get on the road we're all going to die."

Somehow I'd managed to forget about Jerek's mom. Given just how strained their relationship had obviously been, I wasn't sure if it was appropriate to express my condolences. I started to express them anyway, but Jerek waved away my words.

"I'm sorry to put this on you, Dani, but you're the only one who can make this happen. Mother told Thomas to listen to you before she left. It's not much, but that may be enough to allow you to get him moving people down to the boat. You're going to need his help, we're too heavy—especially once we drop into a healing trance—for you to move by yourself."

"How do I know if someone's dead or just in a healing trance?"

Jerek coughed again and I could tell at least one of his lungs was filling up with blood. "If they feel like solid rock, then they're still alive and will probably survive if you can get them out of here."

There was such naked need in Jerek's eyes that I found myself moving despite my shock. I forced myself to my feet and hurried over to where Thomas was looking blankly at all of the bodies strewn across the pool area.

"Thomas, you've got to get Caine and Jerek to the boat down at the dock. We need to make sure we're gone before any more hunters show back up."

He gave me a childish look of confusion. "What about Cyrene? I can't just leave her out there with nobody to help her. Who knows what that thing will do to her."

"Listen, Thomas. She told you to obey my orders. She said that I was picking your targets, that I was the one who understood what was going on here. You need to remember that and continue to obey me. Now, are you strong enough to pick Caine up when he's lapsed into a healing trance?"

Thomas shrugged listlessly. "I just don't understand what happened here. How did you just do that? You shouldn't be able to do something like that at all, let alone be able to produce as much fire as a gargoyle."

I didn't know how to respond to that. I had no more idea how I'd produced a torrent of flame like that than he did, but I sensed that this wasn't the time to be getting caught up in questions that weren't going to matter if we didn't make it to the boats before that hunter elder came back.

"Just get started moving people to the boat, Thomas. I'll tell you what I know once we're safely in a car headed away from Wisconsin. Until then, your only concern is getting Caine and Jerek to the boat. I'll go check and see if anyone else has survived while you do that."

Time moved forward in fits and starts. It took me a depressingly short amount of time to confirm that there was only one other surviving gargoyle out of the entire group of men and women that the queen had brought with her. I touched one bloody person after another and time and time again found them to be limp and lifeless.

Never in my wildest dreams had I expected to be walking through the remnants of a battlefield touching corpses, but I knew Jerek was right. I couldn't just leave one of the warriors behind if they'd somehow survived the fighting and lapsed into a healing trance. There was no way that they would recover before the hunters came back, and I was absolutely certain that the rock-hard skin that was a side effect of their bodies trying to heal themselves wouldn't be enough to save them from hunters with plenty of time and a burning desire to rack up another gargoyle kill.

The only surviving gargoyle other than Caine and Jerek was a girl who looked like she was in her early twenties. She had thick red hair and a gentle face that didn't seem like it belonged in such a violent setting. As I bent down to touch her shoulder I thought that under other circumstances, assuming that my curse didn't cause her to hate me on sight, she looked like the kind of person I could've been friends with. Realizing that she was in a healing trance rather than dead was such a relief that I started crying.

I could see Thomas laboriously dragging Caine down the steps toward the dock, but I just couldn't bring myself to run down there and help him—not as long as he seemed to be managing it. Jerek and Caine had been pretty clear on the fact that the human half of the bond—even when the human wasn't the dominant partner—still gained a measure of the gargoyle's unnatural strength.

When you stacked my puny muscles up against someone the size of Thomas, who also had a metaphysical assist from Jerek's mother, it didn't seem like there was really much I could contribute. Instead of going down and helping Thomas, I wandered back over to Jerek, fully expecting to find that he'd lapsed into a healing trance as well.

He looked up and gave me a shaky smile that was a clear sign of just how close he was to the end of his strength. "Did any of them make it?"

As he asked the question there was a fine tremble to his bottom lip which wouldn't even have been detectable if not for the way his lip ring reflected the lights from the house.

If I'd had any remaining doubts about Jerek, that one question would've settled them. Caine was right. Jerek pretended to be remote—tried to convince everyone around him that he didn't care about anyone else—but the truth was that was nothing but a defense mechanism. Everything Jerek had done since we'd been attacked the first time had been because of how much he cared.

He'd assessed the situation just like the crown prince he was, and then he'd acted under his own initiative when his mother had refused to believe that the hunters here in Wisconsin were so much more dangerous than any his race had ever encountered before. He'd been willing to sacrifice his life if that was what was required to make sure that his mother brought a big enough force to handle the size of the incursion he'd been worried about.

There was always the possibility that his empathy and concern for people only extended to his own kind, but I just couldn't bring myself to believe that. Someone willing to sacrifice so much, someone who'd been willing to sacrifice everything for me, wasn't the kind of guy who viewed humans as nothing more than a disposable commodity. Jerek was the real deal, and if nothing else good came out of the massacre we'd just gone through, I told myself that at least I understood his true character, and in some ways that understanding was priceless.

"There's one, a girl who looks like she's a few years older than us. She's got red hair, and she looks like she was never meant for this kind of life."

Jerek nodded wordlessly as the reality of our losses were confirmed. "You need to get down to the boat right now, Dani. Take Thomas' phone so you've got the ability to call my father, and get the boat started. If the hunters come back before

Thomas manages to get all of us down to the dock, then you need to drive away and call my father. He's not going to want to believe you, but you've got to make him believe you. Everything depends on it."

"I'm not driving off without you. Come on, let's get you down there so you can lapse into a healing trance. I don't like how pale you've gotten."

"It'll never work. I don't have very much longer before I'll have lost too much blood for even a healing trance to save me. You need to save yourself, but before you go there is one thing I need to tell you."

"Stop it, just stop it. I'm not leaving you or Caine, or even the redhead chick. If you need to go into a healing trance then go into a healing trance, but if you've got enough strength left to be telling me something, then save that and help me get you down to the dock. I'll drag you if I have to."

Jerek coughed again, but he nodded and let me help pull him to his feet. He was a lot lighter than I'd been expecting, almost as though all the blood he'd lost had shrunk him down to the point where he was as light as a normal guy our age would've been. It was one more reason to worry about him, but I had to just trust that he would know when he needed to go into a healing trance in order to heal himself of all of the damage he'd sustained.

I would've just told him to enter a healing trance, but I knew I wouldn't even be able to budge him once that happened, and I really was worried about being forced to leave him behind. Despite my brave words to the contrary, I finally understood the stakes. If it came to a question of staying there with Jerek and dying by his side, or warning the gargoyle nation that they had a dangerous hunter infestation growing in northern Wisconsin, I would choose to save the thousands of people who were otherwise going to be carried through to the other side of the portal to serve as some kind of awful, renewable food source.

I wrapped Jerek's left arm over my shoulders and tried to support him around the waist with my right arm, but it was a lot more difficult than I'd been expecting. The gargoyles were every bit as fireproof as I'd been led to believe, but the same couldn't be said of their clothes. Between the fire unleashed by Thomas and the queen, my own contribution to the battle, and the damage done by the hunters' razor-sharp claws, none of the gargoyles were wearing as much in the way of clothing as they'd started out with.

Jerek basically looked like the Incredible Hulk in the clothing department. He still had pants on, but they were little more than tatters below the knees, and his shirt had burned right off of his body when I'd saved him from the last few hunters.

Between that and all of the blood, it was surprisingly difficult for me to get a grip on him with my right hand. I finally settled for grabbing him by the belt as I half carried him down toward the dock.

STONE HEART

About a third of the way to our destination, we passed Thomas, who'd successfully gotten Caine into the boat and was headed back toward the house. I asked him to pick up the redhead and bring her down as well, and then focused on keeping my knees from buckling as I was forced to support more and more of Jerek's weight.

By the time we made it to the boat, I wasn't entirely sure that Jerek was still conscious. I half dropped him into the bottom of the boat simply because I wasn't strong enough to lower him in as gently as I would've liked to, which drew a groan out of him. That eased my concerns that he'd lost consciousness without making it into the healing trance that was his only chance of surviving long enough for us to get him across the lake. I had no idea if it was possible for a gargoyle to lapse into a healing trance out of some kind of reflexive, self-preservation instinct while they were unconscious, but the last thing I wanted now was to lose him after finding out that there really was more to him than the facade he presented to the outside world.

I climbed into the boat after him and straightened out his arms and legs before grabbing a life jacket to serve as an improvised pillow. "Jerek, you're in the boat and I'm about to turn on the engine. Go ahead and let yourself drop into a healing trance. There's no reason to continue fighting it, and the sooner you start letting your body repair itself, the sooner you'll

---

be awake again and able to tell Thomas and me what to do."

Jerek coughed again, and I got the feeling that the only reason his lungs hadn't filled completely with blood was that there was no longer enough pressure inside his circulatory system for that. "No, I can't do that until I've come clean with you."

He reached weakly toward me, and I met him halfway, taking his hand in mine. I hadn't expected that to make any kind of difference—I wasn't even sure he was still with it enough to register the fact that we were touching—but it was like some of the tension and pain instantly drained out of him.

"Go ahead and tell me. Whatever it is, it can wait, but if that's what it will take for you to take care of yourself go ahead. I just want you to get better."

"This isn't the first time we've met, Dani."

"Of course it isn't. We met a couple of days ago when you threw the party at your house." I was half convinced that he was delusional, but he squeezed my hand with surprising strength.

"No, we met four or five years ago. My gift had just started to work reliably and you were the most amazing person I'd ever seen. I didn't know how else to protect you, so I did the only thing I could think of. I bonded you. Without you ever even knowing what had happened, I completed the first phase of the bond and I've been fighting your pull ever since."

Acknowledgements

2015 hasn't gone at all like I planned. In some ways that's been good, in others it's been a massive disappointment. One of the biggest disappointments has been the way that marketing has gotten into the way of writing. My initial production schedule had Stone Heart coming out months earlier, but given all of the unexpected developments in 2015 and some happenings in 2014 that proved to be more impactful than I initially realized, I consider myself fortunate to have been able to push forward with things as well as I did.

I'm incredibly grateful for the help of a number of people in bringing Stone Heart to life. As always, my editors (Amy Jirsa-Smith and RJ Rocksley) both did exemplary work when it came to whipping my rough draft into something with far fewer errors than the version I handed them—thank you both!

My advance readers continued to provide helpful feedback and proofing for Stone Heart, and I'm grateful to all of them for their ongoing help and support. In no particular order they are: Mom, Dad, Matthew, Shalese, Lachele, Mark, Kim, Janelle, Jenine, Mei and Heather.

I would also like to express thanks to Merissa at http://archaeolibrarianologist.blogspot.com/ for her ongoing efforts to get the word out about my books, all of the members of my Launch Team (you guys and gals are awesome), and all of you readers who take the time to tell your friends and family about my books.

Finally, as always, the biggest thanks goes to my wife, Katie, who in addition to being generally amazing, serves as my cover designer, first reader, and confidant. Taking the rough draft of Stone Heart through to a finished product was the start of a particularly trying time for me professionally and I couldn't have continued doing what I do without her help. Thank you Katie!

About the Author

Dean Murray is a prolific author with dozens of titles across multiple pen names and more than half a million copies of his work currently in circulation.

Dean started reading seriously in the second grade due to a competition and has spent most of the subsequent three decades lost in other people's worlds.

Things worsened, or improved depending on your point of view, when he first started experimenting with writing while finishing up his accounting degree. These days Dean has a wonderful wife and two lovely daughters to keep him rather more grounded, but the idea of bringing others along with him as he meets interesting new people in universes nobody else has ever seen tends to drag him back to his computer on a fairly regular basis.

Keep up to speed on Dean's latest projects at deanwrites.com.

The Society

People need to be monitored, or they'll repeat the mistakes of the Desolation, a centuries-old war that killed billions of people and destroyed civilization.

Skye is part of the Society, the hi-tech, nanite-endowed group responsible for making sure that the millions of surviving people—grubbers—are confined to the ancient, decaying cities where they can be watched to ensure they aren't redeveloping the weapons technology that came so close to extinguishing life on the planet.

When the Society's monitoring programs pick up troubling developments in one of the grubber cities, Skye is ordered in to deal with the man responsible, but what—and who—she finds once she arrives will change everything.

Reborn

True love never dies.

A new arrival at Selene's high school is about to turn her entire world upside down. She's never met anyone so attractive—or so mysterious—before this, but Jace's unyielding insistence that they've known each other for decades can't be denied—not given how familiar he feels to her.

In the hidden world of gods and fairies what you don't know can get you killed faster than anything else and only those you love have any chance of saving you.

Broken

Adri Paige's arrival in Sanctuary thrusts her into a dangerous, shadowy world most people don't believe exists, and places her in the middle of a war between darkly handsome Alec Graves and charismatic Brandon Worthingfield that threatens to consume the entire town.

On the surface, both Alec and Brandon are nothing more than average high-school guys, but as Adri is pulled ever more deeply into their conflict she realizes that one of them wants to kill her. Adri needs to decide who to trust before her time runs out once and for all.